NIGHTS OF

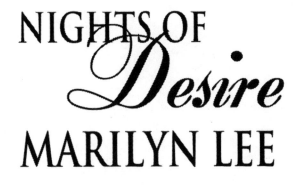

Desire

MARILYN LEE

ELLORA'S CAVE
ROMANTICA PUBLISHING

An Ellora's Cave Romantica Publication

www.ellorascave.com

Nights of Desire

ISBN 9781419958465
ALL RIGHTS RESERVED.
Nights of Desire Copyright © 2007 Marilyn Lee
Edited by Helen Woodall.
Photography by Les Byerley.
Cover art by Syneca.

This book printed in the U.S.A. by Jasmine–Jade Enterprises, LLC.

Electronic book Publication August 2007
Trade paperback Publication November 2008

Excerpt from *Love out Loud* Copyright © Marilyn Lee, 2008
Excerpt from *Full BodiedCharmer* Copyright © Marilyn Lee, 2002

NIGHTS OF DESIRE

ജ

Chapter One

ဆ

For several minutes after she woke, Tempest Marshall lay with her eyes shut tight. She took several slow, deep breaths. They didn't help. When she opened her eyes again, she was still naked. There was still an equally nude male body curled against her back in the strange bedroom. A large, warm palm still cupped her right breast.

She swallowed slowly, struggling to remember the events of the previous night. What had happened after her second drink? How had she ended up in bed with a man? She frowned. A vague memory of a slightly raunchy slow dance with Layton hovered at the edges of her confused thoughts.

Her cheeks burned as the events of the night before slowly evolved. After a moment of panic, she took a deep breath, closed her eyes and allowed the memories of the previous night to rush over her.

Tempest finished her drink and set her glass down on the large coffee table in front of the sofa where she sat with her best friend, Benai. She glanced around the huge dimly lit room until she spotted the tall, handsome figure of her boss. Dressed in a dark, tailor-made suit that emphasized the breadth of his wide shoulders, his narrow hips and long legs, Layton was more breathtaking than usual.

His thick, dark hair, worn short in the front and on the sides and just below collar length in the back, provided the perfect frame for his tanned face with its high cheekbones. Although he was hosting the annual company party, he stood alone, slowly surveying the people gathered in his living

Marilyn Lee

room. This year's theme, chosen by Tempest, was Countdown to Valentine's Day.

He turned his head suddenly. As he locked his dark brown gaze on her, his firm, sensuous lips curved in a slow, intimate smile.

Tempest's heartbeat increased. She tore her gaze from his and noted the sprig of mistletoe dangling above the large double doors to his right.

As if in concert with the small, inner voice that whispered it was now or never, Benai leaned close. "The rumor about him keeping the kiss-me-now-twig hanging around all year is true."

"I guess so."

"But where're all those handsome brothers of his?"

The Grayhawks were a close-knit family. Over the years Tempest and Layton had worked together, Tempest had met each of his many siblings several times. Usually one or more of them made at least a token appearance at all of his parties.

"I don't know but I'm surprised you've never met any of his brothers."

"There's never really been an occasion for me to meet any of them." Benai gave an exaggerated sigh. "It's just my luck that the only hunk here tonight is yours."

Tempest shook her head. "He's not mine."

Benai shrugged. "Maybe not yet but I have a feeling he could be yours…if you take full advantage of your opportunities and the fact that it will soon be Valentine's Day."

"So?"

"So it's nearly Valentine's Day *and* he's practically standing under mistletoe. "You and I are about the only women here who haven't kissed him. Am I going to make a move on him or are you?"

"Stay away from him, girl."

10

"Then get your butt in gear and go engage him in a lip lock he'll still be thinking about this time next year."

Tempest cast a quick glance at the clock on the mantel. Eleven thirty-five p.m. In just twenty-five minutes until it would be Valentine's Day. Her usual inhibitions lowered by two highballs, she nodded. "Wish me luck." She stood up. Maneuvering around dancing couples, she crossed the room.

She watched Layton watching her approach. His dark gaze never wavered from hers.

She stopped in front of him. "Layton…" Her voice sounded breathless. She paused and moistened her lips.

He smiled again, revealing even, white teeth. "Finally."

She blinked up at him. "Finally?"

"I was beginning to think you were deliberately avoiding me. I haven't seen you since you arrived two hours ago."

"I was just mingling."

"Ah."

Uncertain how respond to that, she decided to pursue a safe topic—at least for the moment. She cast a quick look around the room. "I'm surprised not to see any of your siblings."

"So am I." He grinned. "It must be my lucky night."

"Where's everyone?"

"Let's see. Randall's out of the country. Declan's at an out of state training conference. Lelia is asserting her independence and avoiding us all. Peyton, Dalton and Jordan are in various places. That leaves Brandon and Bancroft. I'm not sure where they are."

"Oh."

He surveyed her, his eyes lingering on the bodice of the mahogany silk dress she'd bought for the occasion. "You look…"

The dress had cost far more money than she usually spent on a single clothing item but both she and Benai had agreed it

11

complimented both her dark skin tone and her figure. Did Layton agree? "Yes?"

He looked in her eyes. "Lovely."

She smiled. The dress had been worth every penny after all. "So you like my dress? It's new."

"Your dress? It's new?"

"Yes. I'm glad you think it's lovely."

"I wasn't talking about the dress."

"But you said it looked lovely."

"No. I said you look lovely." He surveyed the dress again, this time allowing his gaze to linger in her hip area before looking into her eyes. "The dress is nice but you look stunning—as usual."

She caught her breath, feeling her cheeks grow warm. No man other than Brian had ever called her lovely so she suspected Layton was being kind, or maybe he'd had one too many. Either way, she intended to take advantage of what might be her last opportunity for a brief fling with him. She dragged her tongue along the curve of her lips. "So do you."

He arched a brow. "You think I look lovely? Try again."

She laughed and shook her head. "Okay. You look…handsome."

"That's better. Now, tell me, Tempest, do I look handsome enough to kiss under the mistletoe?"

Her stomach churned and her heartbeat raced. "Yes," she whispered.

"So? Are you going to keep me waiting all night?"

"You want me to kiss you?"

"I'm not hanging around this damned mistletoe because I have nothing better to do."

She studied his mouth. He had a firm, sensual bottom lip and a short upper lip.

"Are you going to kiss me or just stare at my lips all night?"

"If you want to be kissed, I—"

"I do."

"Won't Cheryl object?"

"She's not here nor has she any standing to object. Do you have any more objections or stalling tactics?"

"No."

"Then bring those sweet lips of yours over here."

She leaned close and kissed his cheek.

"Kiss me," he whispered.

"I just did."

When she would have stepped away from him, he cupped a hand over the back of her head. "I meant a real kiss." He turned his head and their lips met.

A jolt of pleasure shot through her. She trembled, pressing closer. When he slipped an arm around her waist, she parted her lips and ran the tip of her tongue along his mouth. His arm tightened around her, forcing her body closer to his.

With her hands pressed against his shoulders, she leaned into him. Within seconds, she was lost in his kiss. She linked her arms around his neck and welcomed his tongue in her mouth. His body felt hard and unyielding against hers. She longed to melt into him and surrender completely to the passion building in her. Afraid she'd embarrass them both by grinding herself shamelessly against him, she quickly stepped back.

He arched a brow and waited for her to speak.

She swallowed several times before she parted her lips. "Good."

He shrugged. "Was it? It was a little on the short side. We'll need to do it again to be sure."

She blinked at him. "You're flirting with me."

"Yes. I know. What do you plan to do about it?"

She extended her hand. "Will you dance with me?"

He smiled. "I thought you'd never ask." He placed his big hands on her waist. He drew her close until she felt molded against the hard muscles of his big, sculptured body.

She shivered, placing her hands against his chest. She felt the steady beating of his heart. Anticipation raced along her nerve endings. This wasn't the first time they'd danced but she was going to do her best to ensure this particular dance was special.

He sighed. "Too close?"

After that kiss? And after years of secret fantasies too intimate to share even with Benai? She slid her hand up his chest and linked her arms around his neck. She rotated her hips against his, determined to do her best to ensure they ended up in bed. "Not nearly."

His smile widened. "I was hoping you'd feel that way."

She brushed her fingers through the hair at the nape of his neck. "I do."

He bent his head until his lips nearly touched her ear. He spoke in a low, husky voice. "Please tell me you're sober enough to know what you're saying and implying."

She moistened her lips.

He brushed his lips against her ear. "Tell me quickly…while I'm still capable of walking away from you."

Oh the possibilities suggested by his words. What wouldn't she give to have him out of control and wanting her? "I am." She leaned her upper body away from his and met his dark gaze. "Are you?"

"I was—until you asked me to dance. Now I'm feeling downright high."

There was no mistaking his meaning. She wanted to make her own desires equally clear. She deliberately licked her lips. "I know the feeling, Layton."

"Damn, I like the way you say my name in that soft, breathless voice."

"I like you," she told him.

He inhaled quickly. "Flirting is fine but if you keep this up, I'll expect you to follow through. If all you're interested in is a dance, now's the time to stop flirting, Tempest."

She slowly rotated her hips against his. "Does this feel like all I want is a dance?"

He stared down into her eyes. "Tempest?"

"I want far more than just a dance, Layton."

"Really?"

She nodded. "Dancing with you is...exhilarating but I want to share more than this dance with you tonight, Layton."

He kept his hands on her waist and his groin pressed against hers as they slowly swayed to the music. "How much more than a dance are you interested in?"

Her heartbeat increased. She took a deep breath before she replied. "Everything."

"Everything...as in *everything*?"

"Yes and I want it all night."

"Everything? All night?"

He sounded surprised. She blushed. "Have I shocked you?"

His fingers tightened around her waist. "Shocked? No. Aroused? Oh yeah."

"So you're...interested?"

He slid his right hand down from her waist to quickly brush against her ass. "Hell, yeah and we can share everything, all right...if you're sure you're sober."

"I've had less than two drinks. I'm sober and I know I'd like to spend Valentine's Day...in bed with you." There. She'd finally admitted she wanted him to be more than a professional friend—at least for the coming night.

His looked at her lips. "Damn, Tempest. Are you sure?"

Feeling the blood rush up to her cheeks again, she lowered her gaze and pressed her cheek against his shoulder. "I've haven't been surer of anything in a very long time." She wrapped her arms around his waist. "So we're going to spend the night together?"

When he didn't respond immediately, she lifted her head. "Layton?"

He remained silent, staring down into her eyes.

Why didn't he say something? Anything? Oh hell. "You're not going to make me beg. Are you?"

His firm, sensual lips curved up in a small, intimate smile. "Would you?"

She released her hold on his waist and slid her palms over his chest. "Oh Layton. Please don't do this to me."

His smile vanished. He brushed her cheek. "Don't misunderstand, Tempest."

"What? What am I misunderstanding?"

"The music's stopped and people are beginning to stare." He sighed. "We'll have to continue this conversation later."

She licked her lips and met his dark gaze. During the eight years they'd worked together, their relationship had gradually evolved from a straight employer-employee one to what she privately thought of as one of "professional friendship." They frequently had lunch out and they shared several non-business related dinners a year. They'd even slow danced a few times at various parties. He sent her an elaborate bouquet on her birthday and on what he called just-because occasions several times a year.

When she had asked him why he'd sent the first bouquet, he'd just arched a brow and given her an enigmatic smile that had made her heart pound. He had always shown a casual interest in her dating status. Nevertheless, he had never given her reason to suspect he had any personal interest in her. In fact, he'd always gone out of his way to introduce her to what she had privately come to think of as his latest conquest. He'd even been known to ask her advice when he wanted to buy his current fling a present.

She understood his lack of interest in a personal relationship with her. Why would the CEO of a successful medical supply company want to romance his plain Jane soon to be ex-chief accountant? Each of his post-divorce dates had been a beauty. A Native American male, he'd shown a marked preference for tall, gorgeous, big-breasted, brown-eyed blondes with long, flowing hair. She was tall and had large breasts. However, her brown eyes were nondescript. She wore her dark brown hair in a mass of short, permed curls.

"That's not necessary. I get your point."

"I doubt it but judging by the way everyone is staring at us, we'll definitely be the topic of office gossip at work on Monday." He sighed again, glanced around the room and abruptly released her. "I need to mingle."

She sucked in a painful breath. Why couldn't his second thoughts have come *before* he'd allowed her to make a fool of herself? Thank God her resignation from the company would be final in two weeks and she wouldn't need to face him again. Since she'd be starting her own small accounting business operated from the home she'd inherited from her father, there would be no danger of running into him while working.

She nodded and turned away. "Fine."

"Tempest?"

She shook her head. "It's okay, Layton. You don't have to say anything else. I understand."

"Tempest!" He caught her hand.

She reluctantly turned to face him, keeping her gaze on his chin. "I said I understood."

"I can see from the hurt look on your face that you don't."

She bit her lip and remained silent, afraid to trust her voice.

He surprised her by stroking his fingers against her cheek. "Tempest? Look at me."

She lifted her gaze to his.

He smiled. "That's better. Now stop jumping to erroneous conclusions."

"I don't understand."

"You will—when we continue this conversation later when we're alone."

"I don't...understand."

"You're repeating yourself." He squeezed her hand. "The sooner we circulate, the sooner we can get rid of everyone else. Then we can talk without interruptions."

She saw the clear desire in his gaze. Her confidence returned. "Talk? When we're alone you want to talk?"

He shrugged. "Ok. I want to do more than talk."

"So do I."

"Good. It's a date, then." He released her hand.

She nodded. "Yes."

"I suppose it would be too rude to just tell everyone to get the hell out of here so we can be alone."

"Yes it would."

He shrugged. "Well, I have been known to be rude—from time to time and I'm sure everyone would quickly recover and delight their friends with lurid tales of the night I lost my head over you."

"Layton, you're going to make me blush again."

"You'll be doing more than blushing by the time the night is over."

She caught her breath. "You were going to mingle."

"I'd rather mingle with you."

"Hold that thought." She smiled and made her way back to the sofa where Benai waited. Tempest sank down beside her and sighed.

After a moment, Benai elbowed her. "Well?"

Tempest turned to face her, feeling a smile spread across her face. "Oh Nai, I think he's interested!"

"You think?"

She shook her head. "I know he's interested."

Benai grinned. "Well, don't expect me to act surprised. Haven't I been telling you for the last two years that he's been sending you a message with those expensive bouquets he's always finding excuses to send you?"

"Yes but—"

"And how many times has he chosen to drive on business trips when flying would have been far more convenient?"

Tempest shrugged. "He likes to drive."

"Really? How come he only drove when you were accompanying him? Can you name one business trip he made by himself where he drove?"

"Yes. When he…well there was the time when…" she trailed off.

Benai nodded. "I thought not. Remember, I'm his personal accountant."

"I know but I never once thought you might be right."

"Well, clearly I was. So what are you doing sitting here with me instead of slow dancing with him?"

"He wants us to mingle."

"Hmmm. And then?"

Tempest shrugged. "And then we'll see." She rose. "Right now I'm going to mingle."

Benai nodded. "You go, girl!"

Tempest moved through the throngs of people. She stopped frequently to talk to co-workers but she was always aware of Layton, on the opposite side of the room. Just before midnight, he joined the group she stood with. As the

19

countdown started, he linked his fingers through hers. The clock struck midnight. He squeezed her hand.

She smiled up at him. "Happy Valentine's Day, Layton."

He bent his head and brushed his lips against hers in a brief but sweet salute. "Happy Valentine's Day, sweetheart."

He whispered the words against the corner of her mouth. She leaned into him, her stomach muscles tightening. "Layton, I—"

"My turn."

Feeling a hand on her shoulder, she turned and lifted her face. One of her male co-workers bent and kissed her cheek before urging her into another pair of arms. A round of causal kissing and social hugging ensued. By the time Tempest had been kissed and hugged so many times her cheek felt numb, she found herself near a love seat by the patio doors. Benai sat on one cushion seat talking with one of the junior accountants in Tempest's department. She smiled at them both.

Benai rose and kissed Tempest's cheek. "Dave's giving me a lift home."

She and Benai had come in her car. Since they'd discussed Tempest's hopes for the evening on the drive to Layton's mansion, Benai had been the designated driver and Tempest had planned to give Benai the keys to her car at the end of the evening.

She glanced at Dave, trying to recall if she'd seen him drinking.

He shook his head. "Don't worry. I'll drive. Paul, Hal and I take turns driving when we go out. Tonight was my night to go dry. I'll make sure Benai gets home safe and sound."

She smiled. "Thanks, Dave." She turned back to look at Benai. "I'll talk to you tomorrow."

Benai hugged her and whispered in her ear. "Rock his world."

"I plan to." She stepped away from Benai and watched her, Dave and the two other junior accountants say goodbye to Layton.

A succession of people waved to her as they left. An hour later, she and Layton were alone in the room. He joined her on the love seat, sitting half facing her with his arm along the back of the seat. "Hi."

If things went as she hoped, Layton would be the only lover who had touched her emotions since Brian. Shyness warred with anticipation. Shyness won. She lowered her gaze. "Hi."

He slipped a finger up her chin and lifted it. "Are you having second thoughts?"

Hearing the tension in his voice, she lifted her lids. Uncertain what emotion she saw in his dark, intense gaze, she bit her lip. "Are you?"

"Have you ever heard of a country song called 'Every Second'?"

She pretended to shudder. "You know I only listen to country music when you force it on me."

He laughed. "It's the music of love."

"Sure it is."

He pressed a finger against her lips. "In the song when the man is responding to a question as to whether he's having second thoughts about their relationship, he responds by telling his woman he has them about her every second, every minute, every hour of every day. Those lyrics just about sum up how I'm feeling right now about you and what's about to happen between us. Like his, all mine are good ones and all centered on you."

She stared at him, her eyes misting.

He leaned forward and brushed his lips against hers.

She tasted brandy on his warm, sweet lips. "Oh Layton, in my wildest fantasies, I never imagined—"

"Shhh." He touched his mouth to hers in a series of soft, nibbling kisses.

Feeling warmth spread through her, she parted her lips. She slipped her arms around his neck. Sighing slowly, she leaned into him.

Engulfing her in his arms, he settled against the love seat. He drew her across his lap.

The outline of his cock teased her ass. Oh yes! Yes!

Tingles of desire danced down her spine as he cupped a palm over her breasts. She moaned against his lips, feeling his tongue exploring her mouth before sliding between her lips to suck on her tongue.

She felt a jolt of electricity so strong she shuddered, gasped and jerked away from him.

He opened his eyes.

She stared at him in silence.

He caressed her cheek. "What's wrong?"

"I...I..." She licked her lips. "That felt..." She allowed her words to trail off.

"Good?"

"It felt beyond good. It felt...natural."

"Then let's do it again." He reached out and drew her back into his arms, settling her across his lap.

She wiggled her ass against the hard outline of his cock.

He groaned.

She smiled. "You're aroused."

He nibbled the side of her neck and cupped his hand over her breasts. "What makes you think that?"

"I can feel your cock."

"Oh you're going to feel it all right."

She blushed but turned her head until their lips touched. "Oh Layton. I'm so excited." She nibbled at his lips. "Are we really going to do this?"

"Hell yeah but not here." He sat her on her feet, rose and took her hand in his. "Let's go upstairs before you change your mind."

She shook her head. "I'm not going to change my mind."

He lifted her chin and pressed a long, warm kiss against her lips.

She tingled all over.

He lifted his head and stared down at her. "This is your last chance to change your mind, Tempest. Think carefully before you answer. Take as much time as you need and then tell me if you're sure you're ready to spend the night with me."

"I don't need any more time. I was sure when I arrived and that hasn't changed."

He released a long, deep breath. "Good because I've waited a long time for this."

"You have?"

He caressed her cheek. "Yes."

She stroked her hands over his chest. "How long?"

He shook his head. "That's a conversation for another time. Right now, I just want to make love to you...unless you can think of something else you'd rather do."

"Not at the moment."

He rubbed his thumb against her lip. "I need you to be very sure about this before we go upstairs."

"Layton! How many times do you want me to tell you the same thing? I'm very sure."

He continued to caress her cheek. "I'm not sleeping with anyone."

"What happened to Cheryl?"

He bent his head and nibbled at her lips. "Cheryl who?"

She pushed against his shoulders and leaned away from him. "Cheryl Wissner. The tall, statuesque blonde you were dating five months ago."

"We're not seeing each other anymore."

So that explained why she wasn't at the party. "Why not?"

"Why are we discussing Cheryl?"

"You're the one who started this conversation."

"I started it to point out that since I'm not sleeping with anyone at the moment, I don't have any condoms."

She took a quick breath and then took the plunge. "That's not going to be a problem."

"Why?" He frowned. "Are you planning to lead me on and then ask me to stop? Because if you are—"

She pressed her finger against his lips. "I'm not! You know me better than that, Layton."

"Then why won't I need protection?"

Even as he asked the question, she could see a hint of excitement in his gaze. She felt certain he knew what she was about to say. Nevertheless, she paused before answering. "You won't need any—not tonight and not with me. You know I want to have a baby."

He nodded slowly. "Yes, I do know that, but do you want to have one now and with me?"

"I can't think of anyone I'd rather have father my child, Layton."

"Oh damn, I was hoping you felt that way." He embraced her, pressing his lips against her ear. "I get chills all over just thinking of making love to you, having you conceive and then watching your belly grow round." He kissed her neck, behind her ear. "I'd love you to have my baby."

She shivered in his arms and slowly rotated her hips against him. "Then take me to bed and we'll do our best to get me pregnant."

She watched his Adam's apple bob up and down. Her heart soared. "Layton? You really do want to spend the night with me. Don't you?"

"Oh sweetheart, you have no idea how much I want that."

"You could show me."

He nodded. "That's the idea."

She pulled out of his arms and slipped her hand in his. "So?"

He led her from the living room into the foyer. There was a staircase on either side of the two-story high foyer. He paused at the staircase on the left. "Shall I sweep you off your feet and carry to my room?"

She pressed her chin against his chest. "That would be nice," she admitted. "But I'm not exactly a skinny Minnie."

He slid his palms over her ass. "I know a few skinny Minnies who would pay a fortune for a round ass like this."

"Flattery will get you everything you want tonight but I'd rather you saved all your energy for making love."

"I can do both," he said.

She smiled, stroking her hands over his biceps. She'd first seen him in swimming briefs four years earlier. They'd been relaxing at the pool of the hotel where they'd been staying during a business trip. The sight of his big, tanned body with the rippling, well-defined muscles had nearly taken her breath away. Her fantasies had started that night.

She knew he worked hard to stay in shape. She didn't doubt he could carry her up to the second floor without getting out of breath. "I'm sure you can, Layton but—"

"I want tonight to be everything you want it to be."

"That doesn't require—"

"Then allow me to indulge one of my fantasies."

"Yours?"

He nodded. "Why do you sound so surprised?"

"Well, I didn't think you—"

"That I had fantasies? I do."

"Yes but I didn't think I was the object of any of them."

He cast a quick glance up the staircase before sweeping her off her feet and up into his arms. "You have a lot to learn about me."

She linked her arms around his neck. "Teach me. I'm eager."

He carried her up the wide staircase. Using his foot, he pushed open the last door on the second floor landing. He carried her into a large bedroom with dark, mahogany furniture before he set her on her feet.

She was in his bedroom and he was going to fuck her— finally. She closed her eyes, breathing deeply in an effort to slow her pounding heart.

"Tempest?"

"Layton…" She swallowed slowly.

Chapter Two

He turned her to face him. "Look at me."

She opened her eyes.

He cupped her face between his palms and bent his head.

She lifted her chin and closed her eyes when his warm, insistent lips brushed against hers. Releasing her face to slip his arms around her, he pulled her close and settled his mouth over hers.

Cradling her in his arms, he licked her lips and swept his tongue into her mouth.

A rage of desire surged through her. She leaned into him, eager to be fucked senseless. She moaned against his lips while she rotated her lower body against his. Her need for him felt like an ache. "Layton? Please."

He released her and stepped back. "I'll do my best to please you."

"Do it now. Please."

He nodded and slowly slid her dress zipper down. As he slipped her dress off her shoulders and over her hips, he dropped soft kisses against her shoulders and neck.

She loved the feel of his warm, insistent lips against her bare skin. Each touch of his mouth sent a tingle down her spine.

Her dress fell around her feet. She stepped out of it and kicked it away.

He lifted his head and studied her in silence, his gaze lingering on her bare pussy before he looked in her eyes. She stood before him, wearing only a bra and thigh-high stockings.

He stared at her pussy for several more long moments.

She resisted the urge to cover herself with her hands. Although she was no beauty, she hoped her long-legged body with its ample breasts and padded ass would keep him interested and aroused.

Without speaking, he opened her front-fastening bra. Her breasts, large and heavy, spilled out. "Damn, Tempest, you have beautiful breasts."

She smiled.

"But then I knew you would."

"You've been thinking about my breasts?"

He shook his head. "Not often. Only every time I see you."

While she digested that heady thought, he removed her bra. Instead of tossing it on the floor with her dress, he slipped it into his pants pocket.

"What are you going to do with my bra?"

"Keep it as a reminder of our first night together."

"First night? That implies there'll be a second night."

He smiled, cupping his hands over her breasts. "Pretty and intelligent."

"When you talk like that, you make me *feel* pretty."

"You *are* pretty." He bent his head, pressing his face against her breasts.

"Oh Layton."

He slipped his hands down her body. While he licked and nibbled at her cleavage, he held her hips and ground his groin against her.

She felt his cock straining against his pants. Her vaginal muscles contracted in response. He turned his head and laved her right nipple before he sucked it between his lips. He nipped and gently tugged at it with his teeth until it hardened.

She shivered. "Hmmm."

He kissed his way across to her other breast.

She cupped her hands over his head and pressed her neglected mound against his parted lips. "Hmmm...yes. Oh yes."

He kissed her breast. "Do you like that?"

"Yes."

Cupping his hands over her bare ass, he laved her left nipple with his tongue.

"Hmmm."

He spread his hands over her butt, parted her cheeks and pressed a thumb against her puckered hole.

She gasped and arched her body into his, her pussy flooding.

Dragging his mouth from her breast, he lifted his head. He kissed her. As he devoured her lips, he applied steady pressure against her anus.

"Oh!" A shock of surprised pleasure danced down her spine as his thumb pierced her rear end and slipped inside her.

He inched his thumb deep inside her ass.

A ripple of delight shook her. She wrapped her arms around his neck. She rubbed her breasts against his chest and her wet pussy against his groin while drowning in the sweet heat of the long, demanding kisses that followed.

Aroused and eager to feel his naked cock, she reached between their bodies and fumbled with his waistband button. After she managed to undo it, she unzipped his pants and slipped them down to his muscular thighs.

He stood still.

She pushed his briefs off his hips. His cock sprang upward.

Her heartbeat increased. She cupped her hands over him. His balls were tight and big. His cock felt warm, hard and heavy against her fingers. She stared down at his cock. It would feel wonderful either slowly sliding or wildly surging inside her. She didn't care how it ended up in her, she just wanted his cock deep in her aching pussy. Before that happened, she had another fantasy she'd like to satisfy.

She pulled away from him and pushed his pants down below his knees.

He kicked off his shoes.

She removed her shoes and hose while she watched him undress.

Within moments, they stood facing each other, naked and aroused.

The reaction his swimsuit-clad body had aroused in her was nothing compared to the deep-seated desire she felt gazing at his big, naked body. He was absolutely—

"Beautiful. You are so beautiful, you take my breath away," he told her.

"So is this."

"What?"

"This."

She licked her lips and dropped to her knees in front of him.

He looked down at her. "Tempest?"

"I've wanted to do this for a long time now."

He took a deep breath. "Then be my guest."

Placing her hands on his waist, she leaned forward and kissed the big, dark pink head of his cock. She liked the way it felt against her lips. She cupped one hand under his balls and wrapped the fingers of her other hand around him.

She licked the underside of his thick length, pausing at the base of his shaft to enjoy the light dusting of hair tickling her nose. Then she drew her tongue along his balls before closing her lips over the big head of his cock.

He inhaled sharply and cupped his right hand over the back of her head.

Keeping her lips wrapped around him, she opened her eyes and gazed up at him.

His eyes were closed. The tip of his tongue protruded through his slightly parted lips. He had a pleased look on his handsome face. Smiling, she pumped his shaft and slowly sucked his head. She ran her tongue around his cock and caressed his balls. Soon, she was going to feel him shooting his seed deep inside her.

She closed her eyes and sucked him, drawing several more inches of warm flesh between her lips. He was thick and warm and she loved feeling him sliding between her lips and along her tongue. Nice. So very nice to finally taste and suck him. Feeling the tension build in him excited her. She loved knowing she was quickly pushing him to the brink of orgasm.

"Enough, Tempest!"

In the midst of anticipating the first bursts of his seed shooting into her mouth, she felt him suddenly grip her shoulders.

Her eyes flew open as he pulled her away from his cock. "Layton?" She blinked up at him, confused.

Shaking his head, he lifted her to her feet.

"What's wrong? Was I too rough? Did I hurt you?"

"No."

"Then I don't understand."

"I don't want the first time I come to be in your mouth."

"Why not?"

"Because I want to come inside you."

She wanted that too. She nodded.

He pressed a brief kiss against her lips before he swept her into his arms.

She rubbed her cheek against his chest. "I want you," she whispered.

"You're going to get me." He quickly carried her across the room to the bed.

He stretched her out on her stomach.

She parted her legs. A soft sigh escaped her lips. She closed her eyes and wiggled her hips as his fingers probed her pussy.

"You're wet."

"And so ready for you."

"Here I come." He lay on top of her, linking his fingers through hers.

She felt his cock against her ass. An involuntarily shudder shook her.

He kissed her ear. "I'm going to make love to you now."

Her stomach muscles fluttered. "I want…I need to be fucked first, Layton."

He nibbled at her neck. "Are you sure?"

"Yes! Stop asking me if I'm sure and do it. Please."

He laughed and lifted his body off hers.

She rolled onto her back, parting her legs.

Kneeling between her thighs, he kissed her pussy.

She lifted a foot and pressed it against his shoulder. "That feels very nice but I'm as wet as I can get and I need to be fucked now. Please, Layton, no more foreplay. Let's do it."

He rose to his knees and pressed his cock against her entrance. "Then I'll fuck you."

She gasped and closed her eyes as he pushed forward. Although she was eager for sex, she liked that he didn't plow into her and start fucking away like there was no tomorrow. There was fucking—as in you're-just-a-piece-of-pussy-so-just-lie-back, baby—and then there was fucking—as in this-is-special-because-you're-not-just-an-easy-lay, baby.

She suspected she was getting the latter fuck from the way he eased into her body. Cupping her breasts, she licked her lips as he pushed his thick, hard length slowly into her.

With an inch or two of his cock remaining outside her, he lowered his hips on to hers. She sighed as he slid the last little bit deep inside her. She shivered and slipped her hands down his back. He had a nice round, taut ass.

Fully sheathed in her, he held himself still. "Tempest?"

She opened her eyes. The warm, affectionate look in his dark gaze sent a delicious shiver of anticipation through her. Yes, he was going to fuck her but he wasn't going to treat her like a nameless piece of ass.

"I've wanted this for awhile, Layton."

"I wished I'd known that."

She caressed his ass. "You know it now."

"Yes. I do." He closed his eyes and lowered his head. He tasted and savored her mouth, licking and nibbling at her lips until she parted them. He lifted his hips, drawing all but the big head of his shaft out of her. Then, as he pushed back into her, he slipped his tongue into her mouth.

A jolt of pleasure shot through her. She clenched her hands over his ass and thrust her hips up toward his. He felt so good. Hungry for more, she ground herself against his groin. She savored the feel of his coarse pubic hair against her shaved pubes.

He placed his hands on the bed near her waist, lifting his body slightly off hers.

She made a soft sound of protest.

He responded by thrusting his hips down against hers, driving his cock deep into her eager, wet slit.

"Oh!"

"Damn, Tempest, you are so sweet."

"I'm yours, Layton. Take me. Take me."

He settled his lips over her and deepened his kiss. As he did, he thrust into her again and again. Each time he bottomed out in her, a shock of delight sizzled through her.

Oh yes! She arched her body, grinding her hips against his. Hungry for a harder, rougher ride, she gripped his shoulders, curled her legs over his thighs and thrust herself along his cock.

Luscious prickles danced along her spine, infusing her body with heat and a burning desire to explode around him. The muscles in her stomach tightened. Her pussy pulsed. A wall of warmth descended and surrounded her. He wrapped his arms around her, devouring her lips. He shortened his strokes, thrusting harder and deeper.

Her toes curled. Good. So good. She moaned against his hard, demanding lips. So damned, fucking good. Sex had never been this wonderful, not even with her beloved Brian. But as with Brian, sex with Layton was all-encompassing. Even as he conquered her pussy and left her clinging to him with a rapacious hunger that threatened to consume her, he touched her inner, deepest emotions.

As the fire in her belly set her ablaze, she exploded and willingly surrendered her heart and soul to the man she'd been fantasizing about for years. He responded by clenching her tightly against him. Grunting against her lips, he shuddered and came inside her. He tore his mouth from hers, pressing his lips against her right ear. With each blast into her, he gasped.

His release, coming so close to her own, intensified her orgasm. She raked her nails down his back and clutched his clenching ass, drowning in the sweet knowledge that he was shooting his seed deep into her fertile, unprotected pussy.

After the last detonation, he groaned and collapsed on top of her. His lips moved against her neck but she couldn't tell if he spoke too softly for her to hear or if he was even speaking at all.

Feeling sated, happy and hopeful, she held him. She enjoyed feeling her breasts crushed under his damp chest. She liked that he was still inside her. Hell, she couldn't think of a single thing about him that wasn't wildly wonderful and exciting.

After several moments of lying on top of her, he sighed, kissed her neck and rolled off her. Without his weight and body heat, she felt cold. That feeling didn't last. He reached out and drew her close, settling his big body against her back. He whispered something incomprehensible against her ear.

She liked the sound of the soft, exotic sounding words. She smiled, wiggling her ass against his groin. "Oh, Layton."

"Tempest." He cupped his palms over her breasts. "My Tempest."

His Tempest. She drifted to sleep with a smile on her face.

Later, while it was still dark, he caressed her awake. "Tempest?"

Yawning, she murmured and turned into his arms. "Layton? What's wrong?"

He caressed her ass. "I need you."

"I'm yours."

He rolled her onto her side. Sliding behind her, he cupped one warm palm over her breast.

She parted her legs.

He slipped a hand between her thighs. "Tempest?"

"I'm willing, but you're big so you need to get me very wet and ready for you." She pressed his hand against her.

Raining moist kisses against her neck, he fingered her until she gushed on his thrusting fingers.

He made a small, pleased sound. "You're very wet."

"And ready."

"Oh Tempest, you are so sweet."

"And I'm yours."

"Damn straight you are."

She rotated her ass against him. "What are you going to do about it?"

He lifted her leg and slid inside her.

She welcomed his length. "You feel so good, Layton."

He rolled her nipples between his fingers. "Do you want to make love?"

"No. I want to be fucked again."

"That's my Tempest."

"Yes. I am yours. Please, take me."

He cupped one hand over her breast, held her hip with the other and took her hard and fast. As he stabbed his cock in and out of her, he grunted against her ear that she was sweeter than he'd hoped she'd be. With his sensual, arousing words of lust and need lighting her fire, she came twice in quick succession.

As she exploded the second time, she cried out his name.

Gripping her waist, he held her still. Then slamming his hips against her, he came, flooding her with his seed.

She tightened her vaginal muscles around him, eager to have his seed seep deep inside her.

When he collapsed against her back, she turned in his arms. He rolled her onto her back and slipped back inside her. She held him, stroking her hands down his damp back.

He buried his lips against her neck, trembling. "Oh hell, Tempest, you are so sweet. You're going to ruin me for any other woman."

She smiled, stroking her fingers through his hair. "Don't talk to me about other women when you're still inside me."

He lifted his head. "There is no other woman."

She couldn't make out the expression in his eyes in the dark room but he sounded sincere and intense.

She placed her palms over his face. "Right answer," she told him and brushed her lips against his.

He responded immediately and they lay sharing soft, gentle kisses until he wrapped his arms around her and rolled onto his back.

She lay sprawled on top of him, still impaled on his cock. She rubbed her cheek against his shoulder.

He caressed her ass. "Are you all right?"

She sighed happily. "I've never been better."

"But you're tired?"

"Yes but tomorrow is another day."

"And?"

"And I want to spend it with you...doing whatever you want me to."

"Sounds like a plan." He pressed his lips against her hair, pulled the cover over their naked bodies and held her close. As she drifted off to sleep, she felt his cock slipping out of her body.

Recalling the incredible physical pleasure she'd experience with the first, sweet slide of his cock into her slick pussy the night before, Tempest gasped and opened her eyes, her heart racing. It couldn't be. Sleeping with Layton had been bad enough but sleeping with him without protection had been beyond insane. Granted, she'd lately begun to worry about her biological clock ticking away while she waited in vain to meet another man she could love half as much as she'd loved Brian. Nevertheless, to behave so shamelessly with Layton had been beyond the pale.

She pushed back the sheet covering them and looked down. A big, tanned palm cupped the dark flesh of her large, milk-chocolate colored breast. Oh God. It was true. She'd slept with Layton! She bolted into a sitting position, pulling the sheet up.

She immediately regretted her impulsive act. As the light blanket settled against her nude form, it revealed his. He had an exquisite body with wide shoulders, an impressive chest with a sprinkling of dark hair, six-pack abs, long, runner's legs and a set of big balls that cushioned a dark pink cock that, even dormant, roused her desire.

Her gaze swept up to his handsome face. At forty-one, he reminded her of a combination of a young Timothy Dalton and an even younger Mel Gibson. Like Mel Gibson, he had a smile that made women melt. Like Timothy Dalton, he projected an air of mystery that she'd always found alluring.

During the four years since his divorce, she had seen numerous women shamelessly vie for an opportunity to share his bed. Even after she had begun fantasizing about sleeping with him, she had never actually expected to end up in bed with him.

She lifted her lids and licked her lips as she gazed at his sleeping body. Each time they met for the next two weeks, she was going to be hard-pressed not to remember how good he looked nude and how wonderful his cock felt sliding in and out of her flooded pussy.

Layton murmured softly.

Tempest tensed and then bit her lip as he abruptly opened his eyes and sat up.

Chapter Three
ඉ

He turned his head and stared into her eyes. He held her gaze hostage for several long, breathless moments.

Unable to glance away, she stared back.

He finally glanced down at himself before looking at her again.

Sunlight streamed into the bedroom though partially open vertical blinds. Although her cheeks burned, she didn't look away. The time for modesty had been the previous night *before* she'd allowed him to undress her and take her to bed knowing he had no protection.

He settled against the headboard, his shoulder touching hers. He reached for the end of the blanket and tossed it over his groin. "Damn. I'm beat."

The night before, lying on his side behind her with one hand cupping her breast and the other stroking her clit, while he slammed his long, thick cock balls deep into her pussy, he had whispered, "Damn. You're so sweet, "in that warm, sexy baritone of his.

She tightened her grip on the top of the blanket covering her breasts and stared at his profile. Was that all he had to say to her after a night of giving her multiple climaxes?

He turned his head and met her gaze again. He brushed the back of his hand against her cheek. "Happy Valentine's Day."

She forced a smiled to her lips. "Thanks. Happy V-day to you."

"Are you all right?"

She shrugged. "Yesterday we were boss and subordinate."

He shook his head. "We haven't been just boss and subordinate for a very long time, Tempest."

"Okay. We were friends too yesterday."

"I'd argue that we were more than that as well."

"You would? Why?"

"Why do you think?"

She thought of the numerous meals they'd shared. After many of those meals, she'd often wished he'd kiss her on her lips instead of her cheek when he took her home. She shrugged. "Whatever we were, we became more than I'd expected."

"Does that have to be a bad thing?"

"I don't know. I'll guess I'll know for sure after I recover from the shock of waking up naked in your arms."

"The shock?" He half turned toward her. "Do you regret last night?"

She moistened her lips. "If memory serves, you didn't use…we should have used protection."

"I didn't have any."

"Why not?"

"As I told you, I'm not sleeping with anyone and I wasn't looking for or expecting to sleep with anyone last night so there was no need to have any protection. The lack of a condom didn't seem to be an issue for you last night. In fact, it seemed like a plus." He stroked his fingers along her cheek. "Is it a minus now?"

She blushed. "I wasn't exactly thinking clearly last night."

He sighed. "So you do regret last night?"

She'd never come more than once with any other lover-including with her beloved Brian. "We probably shouldn't have slept with each other without a few more discussions, but no, I don't regret it."

His dark gaze searched hers. "Are you sure?"

She recalled not only her own luscious, multiple climaxes but his as well. Each time he came inside her, the knowledge that she was fertile heightened her pleasure. "I'm positive but I'm not so sure how you're going to feel when I tell you I...we took a big chance last night and I don't mean STD-wise."

"Ahhh. You mean because you're not on any type of birth control and you're more likely to get pregnant at this time of the month than any other?"

She blinked. "How did you know that?"

He arched a brow. "Damn, Tempest. You don't remember?"

She remembered that slow dance during which they'd both become visibly aroused and the desire filled night that had followed. "Remember what?"

"We didn't just jump into bed last night. Before we did, I repeatedly asked you if you were sure you wanted to sleep with me. You assured me you were. And, as you probably recall, last night was not the first time we've discussed our mutual desire for a child without all the romantic entanglements of marriage and so-called committed relationships."

She experienced a prick of dismay at his view of committed relationships. "I know we discussed it when we worked late several weeks earlier but—"

"But?"

"But we discussed it in general terms-not with the intent of sleeping with each other."

"We did that last night."

"But I'm not on birth control."

"You're starting to repeat yourself, Tempest. I knew that last night."

"And you…slept with me anyway?"

He grinned, revealing even, white teeth. "Apparently so."

She flashed him a brief smile. "I've asked brighter questions, haven't I?"

"You have."

"Why did you sleep with me, Layton?"

"You mean besides the fact that you're an attractive, sexy woman and dancing with you got me hot and aroused in record time?"

She blinked. Brian had frequently called her beautiful but she'd been his first and only love. She'd often suspected his feelings caused him to view her through rose-colored glasses. Neither of the two lovers she'd had after Brian's death had called her beautiful or attractive.

Each of Layton's post-divorce dates had looked as if they'd just stepped off the cover of a glitzy magazine. Although he had called her attractive the night before, he might have been a little drunk. Confident he was now sober, she decided to take the unexpected compliment from Layton in stride. She smiled. "Yes. Aside from that."

He narrowed his gaze. "Damn, Tempest, don't you remember any of our conversation last night?"

Most of her memories of the previous night centered on the wonderful, satisfying sex they'd shared. "I remember some of it."

He groaned. "Please don't tell me you feel you were too…impaired to give consent."

"I'm not telling you that at all. I had a nice buzz last night but I was not drunk."

"Then how do you explain your lack of memory today?"

She shrugged. "I don't know how to explain it but I do know I knew I was giving my consent. So please don't doubt that."

"Thank God!" He caressed her cheek. "I'd hate to have you think I'd taken advantage of you when you were drunk."

She shook her head. "I know you'd never do that. Besides, you were obviously impaired yourself."

"What makes you think that?"

"You wouldn't have slept with me if you weren't a little drunk."

He parted his lips, started to shake his head but studied her in silence instead.

She waited a moment. When he remained silent, she glanced at the clock. Ten twenty a.m. She rarely slept past eight a.m. on the weekends but then she hadn't spent so many hours making love in years. "I'd better get up and get dressed."

He tugged gently at the cover over her breasts. "Why?"

She tightened her grip on the blanket. "It's after ten."

He peeled the fingers of one hand away from the blanket. "On a Saturday."

She tightened her remaining fingers around the cover. "I know but I have—"

He shook his head. "You told me last night you had no plans for today and implied you intended to spend most of the day it in bed—with me."

She blushed at her lack of shame the previous night. "Well, I didn't get much sleep last night and I—"

He grinned. "And if I have my way, you're not going to get much tonight either."

"We both had too much to drink last night, Layton but now—"

"Now we're both stone cold sober and about to pick up where we left off last night." He peeled her fingers of her other hand away from the blanket, which he tossed aside.

He stared at her breasts for several moments before he caressed them. "Unless, of course, you object."

43

She pressed a hand against his shoulder. "I don't think I do but you should use protection."

"Why would I do that?" He brushed his lips against hers, sending a tingle of desire shooting down her spine.

She leaned away from him. "Because you're sober now."

He rolled her nipples until they pebbled into tight peaks. He smiled when she moaned and stroked a hand down her belly to cup her mound. When she shamelessly parted her legs, he rubbed his thumb against her clit. "Just so there's no misunderstanding, Tempest, I was not drunk last night."

She pushed his hands away and met his gaze. She saw no evidence of deceit in his eyes. "But when you kissed me, I tasted brandy on your lips."

He grimaced. "I hate brandy."

"Then why drink it?"

"I know you like it and I wanted to ensure you enjoyed our first kiss—"

"How did you know we were going to kiss?"

"Why else would I have spent all that time standing under that blasted mistletoe suffering through all those unwanted kisses? I had just about decided I'd have to come drag you under it when you asked me to dance."

She smiled. "That's so sweet but you drank at least three glasses."

"As I might have mentioned before, I have a high tolerance for alcohol. If I were so inclined, it would take an incredible amount to get me drunk. I haven't been drunk in years."

"I don't understand."

"Don't you? Then let me make myself clear. I knew exactly what I was doing last night."

"Then...why did you do it?"

"No matter how many ways you ask that question, the answer isn't going to change." He leaned closer and cupped her pussy again. "Because you're sweet and sexy and I was tired of pretending I didn't want you. What was your motivation?"

She frowned. Had she already admitted he'd been the object of her fantasies? She couldn't recall. If she hadn't, she wasn't going to admit it now. "I don't know."

He caressed her cheek. "Don't you?"

She swallowed. Whatever force or weakness had driven her to sleep with him the night before was now under control. "Last night was…I won't deny that I enjoyed being with you last night and I'll admit that I'd like to sleep with you again but I think we both need some time away from each other before we make that decision."

He sighed and leaned against the headboard. "What do you propose?"

She scooted toward the end of the bed, pulling the cover with her. "I'm going to dress and go home."

"And then?"

"And then? I don't know. All I know is it's difficult to think clearly while we're both naked."

"Would it help if we dressed?"

With the memory of their night of pleasure growing stronger, she doubted her ability to be rational in his presence. "I need some space and time."

"We can't undo last night, Tempest."

"I know and I'm not saying I want to. I don't but last night is going to make working with you for the next two weeks awkward."

"If that's your only objection, you can work from home for the next two weeks."

"That's not my only objection. Layton, I could very well be pregnant."

He smiled. "From your soft, warm, sweet lips to God's ears."

"You've never once even hinted you found me attractive in all the years we've known each other."

"What's your point?"

"Now you expect me to believe you wouldn't mind fathering a child with me?"

"That's exactly what I expect you to believe."

"Come on, Layton."

He arched a brow. "Why else would I ask you out several times a year and send you flowers on your birthday and take a personal interest in who you were dating? Or do you imagine I'm that interested in the lives of all the females who work for the company?"

"I know you don't wine and dine other employees but before last night, you'd only kissed my cheek a few times."

"That doesn't mean I didn't want to really kiss you." He rubbed the thumb he'd pressed against her pussy along her lips. "If you only knew of my many, frustrating nights of desire, you'd take pity on me."

"Your nights of desire?"

He nodded. "That's how I think of the many long, lonely nights, I lay awake wanting you."

She shook her head. "I know how women chase you and I know you've allowed many of them to catch you. There can't have been that many nights when you were alone."

"Maybe it's not chivalrous to admit it but many of the times I lay wanting you, there was someone on the other side of the bed."

"Didn't any of those women please you?"

"Physically? Yes but none of them ever touched anything…real in me. No matter who I was with, I always wanted you. If you knew how many sleepless nights I'd spent lying awake thinking about you, longing to have you lying in bed with me as you did last night, you'd have been afraid of me."

The sincerity in his voice and tone touched her. She picked up his hand and pressed it between her legs. "So what stopped you from telling me how you felt?"

He stroked her slit. "I was married when we met. Despite what Allison believes, after seeing how my father's infidelity practically destroyed my mother, I vowed once I entered a committed relationship, I would never cheat. Marriage is the ultimate committed relationship."

She nodded. "I know that and I believe that too but what if you fell out of love?"

"I have never been unfaithful to any woman with whom I've been in an exclusive relationship. If it were a dating relationship, I'd be honest with her and end it. If I were married...well...that's what divorce is for. For me, cheating would never be an acceptable alternative."

She heard the passion in his voice and believed him. "Why didn't you tell me how you felt after your divorce?"

He sighed and dipped a finger into her pussy. "You were dating then. If you'll recall, I asked you about your relationship. You implied it was going well. So I bided my time. We were rarely free of romantic entanglements at the same time. When we were, I had to consider the fact that we worked together. Dating a co-worker who is also a subordinate is always risky. If you ever run into Allison, you might ask her who she thought I was having an affair with."

"You had an affair?"

His nostrils flared. "No, I did not!" He shook his head. "But I could never convince her of that. After a while, I stopped trying. The day you handed in your resignation was bittersweet. While I dreaded the lost of your skills, I looked forward to the opportunity to ask you out—without any pretense of it being even mildly work related."

She wanted to be alone to digest all that morning's surprising revelations, including the delicious one that he'd wanted to date her for years. But when she attempted to move away from him, he caught her hand.

"Where do you think you're going?"

"I told you I was going home."

He shook his head. "Maybe later. Right now I have other plans for you."

Chapter Four

ဢ

She caught her breath but didn't protest when he urged her onto her back on the bed.

He stretched out beside her, brushing his warm lips against the corner of her mouth.

She spoke in a trembling voice, "Layton, we should talk before we do this again."

"We can talk later. Right now I need you."

"It's late. If we do this again…one of your servants might walk in on us."

"All of the house staff know not to enter a closed bedroom. They won't knock either. When a room is unoccupied and available to be cleaned, the door is left open. Now enough with the distractions." He rubbed his palm over her breasts.

A tingle of pleasure danced through her. Despite her doubts, she turned on her side, facing him. "We shouldn't, Layton." Even as she spoke, she stroked a hand across his hip to his ass.

He urged her onto her back again and slid his big, hard body on top of hers. "Right now I need you. Tell me you don't want me to make love to you again and I'll stop."

She licked her lips and stared helplessly up into the dark eyes blazing down into hers. How could she ask him to stop when he'd been the object of her most intimate fantasies for the last few years? She settled her hands on his waist and shamelessly rubbed herself against his semi-erect cock.

He sucked in a breath and settled between her legs. Keeping his cock pressed against her, he lifted his upper body, resting his weight on his extended arms. "Tell me."

She rubbed her palms over his ass. "I want you," she admitted.

A tender smile spread over his handsome face. "Finally." He bent his head and lightly kissed her lips before resting his weight on his extended arms again. "Tell me how you want me."

Uncertain what he wanted to hear, she spoke from the wellspring of her desire. "I want you in me." She moved her hands to his lower arms and gently tugged. "There's no feeling in the world quite like having you in me. I want you...all of you buried deep inside me."

"I don't have a condom but since I know you don't want me to come in you again, I can pull out if —"

She whispered her answer, her heart racing. "No. No. I want you to come inside me. I still want a baby...if you still want to give me one."

He closed his eyes and touched his lips to her ear. "Finally! Do you know how long I've waited to hear you admit that?"

She settled her hands on his shoulders. "I think I admitted it last night."

"You can never admit it enough for me."

"In that case, I'd be very happy to have you father my child." A soft sigh of pleasure escaped her lips as she felt the muscles of his chest against her breasts. "Now show me how much you want me, Layton."

To her surprise, he rolled off her and slid down her body.

She lifted her head and frowned down at him. "Layton?"

"I want to taste you."

Her pussy pulsed. Neither of her last two lovers had given her oral sex. She had been too eager for sex the previous night to allow him to eat her. Now she was eager to have him do it.

He settled between her legs.

She closed her eyes and bit her lip when she felt his warm, eager lips parting the folds of her slit.

He rubbed a thumb against her nether lips. "I've never really liked a shaved pussy but damn, Tempest, I love the look of your bare lips. Without hair, I'll be able to see how swollen they are after we fuck."

The muscles in her stomach clenched. "Oh Layton, you make me so hot."

"You're about to get hotter, honey...and wetter."

She licked her lips and pinched her breasts. "I'm already hot and wet. Make me come."

He drew his lips along her slit. At the top, he parted her folds.

"Oh!" She moaned and arched off the bed as he found her clit and gently but relentlessly sucked it.

As he had predicted, within seconds, she was much wetter.

He made sweet, satisfying love to her...lavishing her pussy with his tongue...pressing warm, insistent kisses against it...stroking two fingers in and out...in and out. She shuddered. Nice...good...so delicious and sooo good.

He palmed her ass, lifting and tilting her hips as he tunneled his tongue inside her. She licked her lips and closed her legs around him. She was so close to coming. "More...please...please." She thrust herself against his face, her mounting pleasure heightened by the feel of his unshaven face against her bare pubes.

In response to her pleas, he slipped a hand down her ass, located her hole and pressed a finger against it. As he pierced her bottom with his finger, he settled his lips over her clit.

A series of tiny shivers began in the pit of her stomach. They quickly spread down to her pussy before encompassing her entire body. He gripped her hips and kept his mouth and thrusting tongue against her as she blew apart. Wave after wave of delicious release washed over her, pulling her under a wet, warm wall of delight. She drowned in ecstasy.

While she lay shuddering and moaning, aftershocks of delight shaking her body, he pressed a last kiss between her legs. Rising over her, he settled his big, hard body between her trembling thighs.

Feeling his cock pressed against her entrance, she parted her legs and jerked her ass off the bed, eager for penetration. She moaned as he slowly propelled his hard length between the lips of her slit and deep into her body.

He wrapped his arms around her, buried his face against her neck and rocked his hips against hers. She felt the tension in his body and knew he was already close to coming. Slipping her arms around him, she ground her hips against his and matched him stroke for stroke.

She loved how his hard cock felt surging back into her on each downward thrust. Nevertheless, she tightened her vaginal muscles and made him work hard to draw each inch out of her...all so he could plunge back into her...conquering her pussy and stealing her heart.

She smiled and cradled him close to her body, caressing his lower back and ass when he groaned her name and jettisoned blast after blast of seed deep in her.

When he went limp and lay shuddering on top of her, she stroked his shoulders and kissed his hair.

They lay still entangled for several moments before he pressed his lips against her breasts and finally rolled off her. He slipped behind her, licking the back of her neck.

She resisted the urge to curl her body against his and drift into a contented sleep. It was time to leave—while she still could. Turning to briefly kiss his warm lips, she slipped off the bed and wrapped the cover around her body sarong style. "I have to go."

He turned to look at her, his dark gaze searching hers. "When will I see you again?"

He made no effort to cover himself and she found herself staring at his groin. She licked her lips, realized what she was doing and forced herself to look in his eyes instead. "This is all so new and unexpected."

"Didn't you want it?"

"Yes." She smiled. "I did but I never really expected to get it...you."

"Well, you have."

She nibbled at her lip. "Give me a few days and we'll talk."

He raked a hand through his hair. "Then I shouldn't expect to see you before Monday at work?"

"Today's Saturday."

"I know what day it is."

"It's only two days, Layton." She looked around his bedroom and spotted an open door along the opposite wall. "Bathroom?"

"Yes."

She hesitated before she leaned over and pressed a quick kiss against his cheek. "Thanks."

"For what?"

She rubbed her cheek against the light stubble on his face. "For taking me to heights I've never reached before and...for making me feel beautiful."

"Making love with you took me places I've never been before either." He caressed her cheek. "I have news for you, Tempest, you are beautiful."

"You keep that up and I'll begin to believe you mean it."

"I do mean it."

Feeling a rush of warmth spread through her, she smiled and nodded. "I know and that's one of the things that make last night and this morning so unbelievable for me."

"Then what's the problem?"

"It's not every day a woman gets to live her fantasy. I know this is real but it has the feel of a dream. I know it might not make sense to you but I need some time alone to process this…thing with you. Okay?"

"It's not just a thing, Tempest."

She tilted her head and stared at him. "Please, Layton."

He sighed but nodded.

She kissed his cheek again.

As she straightened, he reached out and pulled the cover away from her body.

He smiled. "That's better. Your body is too lovely to hide."

"Oh Layton, I think I'm going to like this…thing with you."

His smile turned into a grin. "I'm counting on that."

Smiling, she made her way into the bathroom.

The centerpiece of the modern room, was a large, white whirlpool bath. She could see numerous recesses that contained jets. She stared at it for a long time, imagining herself sharing it with Layton. If she lay on top of him with his cock piercing her from the rear, at least one of the jets was in an optimal position…if she kept her legs parted, while Layton surged into her and cupped her breasts, a jet of water could hit her clit.

The thought made her wet. She shook her head and turned away from the tub. On the other side of the bathroom was a walk-in shower enclosed with beautiful glass frosted with what looked like gold leaf.

She turned on the water, adjusted the temperature to suit her and stepped inside. When she returned to the bedroom after a leisurely shower with a large towel wrapped around herself, Layton stood by one of the bedroom windows. He looked great in a pair of jeans and a pullover that seemed to cling lovingly to his big, hard, masculine body. His dark hair curled damply around his head so she assumed he'd taken a shower as well.

Her clothes and her handbag lay on the bottom of the unmade, brass bed where she'd spent the night in his arms. As she picked up her clothes, he turned to look at her. "Can I interest you in lunch or a cup of coffee before you leave?"

Although hungry, she feared if she didn't leave soon, she'd be in danger of ending up in his bed again. She needed to weigh the pros and cons of continuing a sexual relationship with him before they slept together again. While she knew what she wanted from him, it was difficult to believe a man who could bed women beautiful enough to be supermodels could want more than occasional, uncommitted sex with her.

"No thanks." She flashed him a quick smile and went back into the bathroom to dress. When she returned to the bedroom after dressing, he'd left the room. After making sure nothing of hers remained in his bedroom, she opened the door.

Finding herself looking into the dark, surprised gaze of one of Layton's many brothers, she gasped. He stood outside the door with his hand raised to knock.

Like Layton, he was tall and handsome with dark, sexy eyes and thick, glossy, nearly black hair. Unlike Layton, he wore his hair drawn back in a band that reached his broad shoulders.

"Tempest!"

"Brandon...hi."

"That's one of the many things I like about you."

"What?"

"Unlike most people, you never mistake me for Croft. Why is that?"

"I don't know. I know you and Bancroft are supposed to be identical twins—"

"We *are* identical twins and you are one of the few non-family members who can tell us apart."

"I don't know how I know you're Brandon and not Bancroft. I just know you are you."

"I have a theory about why you can tell us apart when no one else can. Want to hear it?"

"I...yes."

"It's because of who you are."

"Who I am? What does that mean?"

"Maybe I should say it's because of who you'll soon be."

She shrugged, shaking her head. "That's not any clearer."

"Probably not but you and I'll talk about it after you and Hawk talk."

She grimaced. "Are you capable of not talking in circles?"

He laughed. "I've been told I have my moments. Is Hawk inside?"

She shook her head. "No."

He smiled suddenly, revealing a white, even smile that rivaled Layton's. "You're looking exceptionally lovely."

This seemed to be her day for compliments from handsome, sexy men. "Ah...thank you." She smiled and waited for him to step aside.

Instead, he studied her face in silence for several moments before he arched a brow, much as Layton often did. He glanced over her shoulder into the bedroom.

She tensed. He would notice the unmade bed. She bit her lip. He was going to know she had slept with Layton. She relaxed her shoulders. He'd always been a gentleman with her. He would pretend not to have noticed and she'd leave with what was left of her modesty intact—at least with Brandon.

"So. I see Hawk finally got lucky and had a hell of a Valentine's Day."

"What?" Her cheeks burned and she averted her gaze. "I...ah...will you excuse me?"

He placed a palm on her stomach.

She sucked in a breath and pushed his hand away. "Brandon!"

He brushed his hand against her cheek. "You're embarrassed." He lifted her chin and smiled down at her. "There's no need to be embarrassed with me, Tempest."

He had a deep, persuasive voice, reminiscent of Layton's. But he wasn't Layton and she was embarrassed. "Please, Brandon."

To her dismay, instead of allowing her to past, keeping his palm against her cheek, he placed his other palm against her stomach again.

She felt a non-sexual tingle and watched as his eyes lit up. He sucked in a breath. "Oh. Damn. Hawk got very lucky." Keeping his hand on her belly, he slipped his other arm around her shoulder and hugged her. He pressed a soft kiss against her forehead. "You're going to make him very happy. Congrats."

Uncertain how to react to his intimate touch or his enigmatic words, she pulled away from him.

He smiled at her.

She turned and hurried down the long hallway to the staircase. She'd been in the mansion Layton had purchased after his divorce often enough to know her way around. She made her way to the living room where she found Layton standing at the patio doors with a cup in his hand.

He turned and smiled at her. "Ready to go?"

She nodded, casting a quick glance over her shoulder. "I didn't realize Brandon was here."

He frowned. "Neither did I. I haven't seen him and didn't know he was coming but you know how it is when you're the eldest and your parents are dead. Brandon and the others know that wherever I am, they are all welcome."

"So I noticed."

He tilted his head. "Is that a problem for you, Tempest?"

She cast a quick glance at the large, oil portrait hanging above the huge fireplace. Layton had told her it had been painted from a photograph taken on his mother's sixtieth birthday. It depictured Malita Grayhawk, her long, thick hair nearly completely gray, surrounded by all of her children. Everyone was smiling but Tempest had always been struck by the sadness in the matriarch's eyes.

Nevertheless, the extreme closeness of the Grayhawk family was just as evident. Even though all his siblings were adults, she knew Layton felt responsible to provide a home where each would feel welcome at any time of the day or night. Besides, she was hardly in a position to dictate who came and went in his house. "No. Of course not."

"Then what's the problem? And before you answer I'd like to remind you that Randall has an even bigger house than this one and they're all just as likely to be there as here."

"That wasn't my concern, Layton."

"You're sure?"

"Yes, I am."

"Good. Allison never got along with them."

"Which ones?"

He grimaced. "None of them. So I was afraid you'd have the same problem."

"No. It's just that meeting him like that was embarrassing."

He frowned. "I thought you liked Brandon."

"I do!"

"Then why should meeting him embarrass you?"

"He was standing outside your bedroom door when I opened it. He looked inside and knew we'd slept together."

"Do you care what he thinks?"

Tempest hesitated and decided not to mention Brandon touching her belly. She knew Brandon had not intended any disrespect. She was also uncertain how Layton would react.

"Tempest? Do you care what Brandon thinks?"

"No!" She closed her eyes briefly and shook her head. "Yes. Of course I do. He's your brother."

"He's only one of many. I have more than my fair share of the damned critters." He put his cup down on an end table and crossed the room to her. He cupped a palm over her cheek. "If he's annoyed you, I'll happily kill him and introduce you to one or two of my other, more cultured siblings."

"I have met all of them—on several occasions."

He nodded. "I know. So you know some of my other brothers are far more refined than that big ox, Brandon."

"He's not an ox."

"Never mind that. Do you want me to kill him or not?"

"Layton!"

He smiled and arched a brow. "Or, if you're squeamish, I'll box his impertinent ears for you."

She laughed, resting her hands against his chest. "I think he's a little too big to have his handsome ears boxed."

"Hey! His ears aren't any more handsome than mine."

Noting the desire in his eyes, she smiled and touched his right ear. "No, they're not. In fact, I don't think I've ever seen a handsomer pair of ears than yours."

"Are you flirting with me again, Tempest?"

She licked her lips suggestively and nodded. "Maybe just a little."

He smiled and bent to brush his lips against hers. "Just for that sweet admission, if you like, I'll kick Brandon out on his flat ass."

"You and what tribe, Hawk?"

They turned.

Brandon stood in the living room doorway, watching them.

Layton winked at her before he frowned at Brandon. "God save me from brash younger brothers looking to get their asses kicked. The day I need help handling your ass will be the day I'm six feet under. Now, if you don't mind we were in the middle of a private—"

"Give me a minute and I'll let you get back to your private conversation." Brandon entered the room and smiled down at her. "I've been driving most of the night and I'm going to bed but I wanted to apologize first." He kissed her cheek. "I didn't mean to embarrass you. It's just that I know how long Hawk's been interested in you and when I saw you coming out of his bedroom—"

Tempest blushed and cast a helpless look at Layton.

He responded by clamping a hand on Brandon's shoulder. "If you don't mind, I'll do my own confessing."

"I'm sorry." Brandon engulfed her in a bear hug.

A feeling of warmth replaced her embarrassment. She'd always liked Brandon but had never felt particularly close to him. Now she did. She placed her hands on his back. "It's all right."

He released her. Instead of immediately moving away, he studied her face, gazing into her eyes in silence.

Tempest stared back, feeling as if he were looking deep into her soul and searching out her most guarded secrets. Strangely, she didn't mind.

He caressed her cheek. "If you ever need to talk, you call me. Okay?"

She nodded. "Okay."

"Good." He kissed her cheek, winked at Layton and left the room.

Tempest watched him leave before she turned to study Layton's handsome face with the high cheekbones and the ruddy-bronze complexion. So it was true. Layton really had been romantically interested in her long before the previous night.

He met her gaze. "Why are you smiling at me like that?"

She blinked. "My mind wandered."

"To happy places?"

She nodded. "Oh, very happy places."

He slipped his arms around her waist. "Then stay and we can explore those happy places together."

She leaned into him, brushing her cheek against his. He'd shaved. Although touching him would probably always give her a thrill, she liked how his unshaven face felt against hers. She gave herself a mental shaking. If she kept thinking like that, she'd end up in bed with him again. "That's a tempting offer but I'd better go."

"Would you stay if Brandon wasn't here?"

"Why do you ask that?"

"Because Allison had a real problem with how close we are as a family. She couldn't understand why they all felt as if they could come to our house whenever they wanted. Would that bother you?"

She shook her head. "I've already said no. I think it's great that you're all so close."

"Good but just so you know when I'm dating, they don't just drop in like Brandon did this morning. They always call and let me know first. And none of them actually live here. They all have their own homes or apartments."

"Oh. Well...I'd better go."

"I'll walk you to your car."

She shook her head and kissed his cheek. "I know the way out. I'll get my coat from the foyer closet and see myself out. I'll see you on Monday, Layton."

He nodded and bent to press a warm kiss against her mouth. "Drive carefully, honey."

Honey. She'd always considered the endearment overused and somewhat hackneyed. It sounded sweet and romantic spoken in his deep baritone. She kissed the corner of his mouth. "I will."

Chapter Five
➳

Layton stood at the patio doors in the living room listening to the sound of Tempest's car leaving the driveway.

"So?"

He turned.

Brandon entered the room and stretched out on the sofa.

Layton crossed the room and sank down in a single chair opposite the sofa. "I thought you were going to sleep."

"I am but I wanted to congratulate you first."

"On?"

Brandon yawned. "Her belly felt...occupied."

Layton sat forward. "It did?"

"Yes." Brandon smiled. "Lelia is going to go wild when she finds out."

Thinking of their youngest sibling and only sister, Layton smiled. "Lelia isn't going to find out just yet." He raked a hand through his hair. "Are you sure?"

"Yes. I felt her belly. I'm positive."

"So that's why she was so freaked out after seeing you?"

"I didn't mean to freak her out but when I saw her standing in your bedroom...looking so...satisfied and so...pregnant, I had to touch her."

He arched a brown. "Did you?"

"Yes." Brandon rose, approached his chair and slapped his shoulder. "Congratulations, you finally got really lucky."

He shook his head. "Not yet. She's not ready to believe how I feel about her yet."

"Probably not but you'll convince her. When you do, we'll have a big, old-fashioned Grayhawk celebration."

He looked up and saw the sad look in Brandon's eyes. "Brandon?"

Brandon shook his head. "I was just thinking how happy Mom would have been."

Layton rose and embraced him. "When it's time to celebrate, she'll be there with us in spirit—just as she's always been."

Brandon nodded. "Yes." He sighed and drew away. "You know winning Tempest won't be easy."

"Nothing worth having ever is."

Brandon smiled. "There you go!" He slapped Layton on the back. "Name the little bugger after me, won't you?"

"And tell Croft what when he objects?"

Brandon grinned. "Seniority has its privileges. I'm the elder twin." He crossed the room but turned at the door. "You will remember that there's only one n in Brandon, won't you?"

Layton smiled and nodded. "I'll remember."

"Great. Then go get your woman."

"Oh I plan to."

"But before you do, you should know you're going to need to be patient."

He frowned. "Patient? I've already waited years. I'm not sure how much patience I have left."

Brandon shrugged. "Then you're going to need to dig deep and find some. She's not sure of herself or you. She'll need a little time."

"She's not getting any…and while we're at it, I need our first child to be a girl. Are you sure it's not?"

"What makes you think I know either way?"

"Brandon—"

"I know she's pregnant. I don't know what sex the child will be. But I also know you'd better dredge up some patience...no matter how difficult it might be. You can't force her into an emotional relationship she's not ready for." Brandon pointed at him. "Don't try and force her, Hawk."

Layton swore softly and strolled across the room to stare out the patio doors. He'd always been aware that Brandon knew things he had no logical way of knowing. Hell, he was usually right when he got his feelings. But this time he was wrong. He had to be. Tempest had to have a girl. She also had to be ready for the relationship and commitment he needed from her. Once she knew how he felt, she'd have to be ready.

* * * * *

Tempest discovered a dozen roses outside her apartment door when she arrived home.

The card read,

Happy Valentine's Day. Yours, Hawk.

Hers. Hawk. Considering his track record with women, did she dare trust him to be hers? How many women had he bedded and discarded since his divorce? Did she dare trust her heart to him? Even if he meant everything he'd said and implied—and she'd never known him to be anything but honest—he ran through women like water.

Spending the night with him had taught her that she could fall very hard and fast for him. While she was sure he would never intentionally hurt her, she was certain he'd broken more than his share of hearts.

Given the certainly that she could very easily and unwisely fall in love with him, she'd need to think long and hard before deciding if she dared continued to sleep with him. Still, she smiled as she undressed. Slipping into bed, she lay curled on her side, her thoughts on Layton and the consequences of having slept with him without protection. She wanted a child or two while she was still young enough to fully enjoy them and be an energetic mother. After Brian's death she'd almost given up on falling in love again. Some people only loved once in a lifetime and after seven years of dating, she feared she might be one of those people.

Layton was intelligent, kind, responsible and resourceful. He had worked his way through college in two and a half years and then gone from a junior accountant in the medical supply firm where they both worked, to its CEO within a period of twelve years. He possessed all the qualities she wanted in the man who fathered her son. Yet aside from her sexual fantasies, she'd never allowed herself to think of him as anything other than a professional friend.

She sighed. While he would make an excellent father, he was too close to his siblings to be willing to father a child with her and allow her to raise the child on her own.

Everything about the familiar, comfortable relationship they'd established over the last eight years had changed and was now in jeopardy. Layton had once told her Brandon *knew* things. She remembered Brandon's cryptic words. She stroked her stomach and shivered. She had a bittersweet feeling that Layton's seed had found its target and she was going to end up pregnant with his baby—unless she did something about it.

She sat up and walked into the bathroom. She stared at her reflection. Her eyes were wide and confused. There were steps that could be taken to ensure she didn't end up pregnant. One call to her doctor and she could have a prescription for the morning after pill. Or was it now available without a prescription?

She shook her head and wrapped her arms around her body. "No. No." If she were prepared to have a baby with a stranger, why not have one with a man she knew, liked and respected? It was true Layton and his family would want to be a part of the baby's life but why would that be so bad? Growing up an only child to a widowed father, she'd longed to be part of a large, loving family. Layton and his many siblings would surround her baby with love and affection.

Provided Layton was prepared to abide by the rules she'd set for herself and the father of her child, there was no good reason for not having his baby.

Granted she'd planned on having a black man father her child but she knew Layton would be a good father. If she had a biracial child he or she would need a strong, loving relationship with a committed father. Layton could be that father.

Hopeful Layton's seed had found its mark, she went back to bed and fell asleep.

* * * * *

Several hours later, yawning and stretching, Tempest reached for the ringing phone on her nightstand, keeping her eyes closed. "Hello?"

"Hi, honey."

She sat up, a smile spreading across her face at the sound of Layton's deep, warm voice. "Hi, Layton. The roses were beautiful. Thank you."

"You're welcome. Do you have any plans for tonight?"

"No. I think I'm just going to stay home and chill."

"You're going to spend Valentine's Day alone?"

"I need to be by myself and I haven't really gotten sentimental about Valentine's Day since…in quite a bit."

"Since your fiancé died?"

She swallowed hard, recalling that despite Brian's pleas, she'd chosen to work over time so she could save for their wedding instead of taking the day off and spending their last Valentine's Day together. Of course, at the time she hadn't known it would be their last Valentine's Day. She'd had no way of knowing he would die several months later. It had taken years for her to get to the point of forgiving herself for having chosen work over a day and night with the man she loved. "Yes."

"If Valentine's Day doesn't mean anything special to you, why did you choose it as the theme of this year's party?"

Why indeed? "I'm not sure."

"I am. I think you knew it would be a special night for us."

She shook her head. "Not in my wildest dreams."

He sighed. "We need to talk, Tempest."

She nodded. "Yes. Do you want to do lunch or maybe dinner on Monday?"

"Actually, I've made reservations at Marikos' for tonight."

"Tonight?" She glanced at her clock radio. "It's nearly four-thirty, Layton and I don't have anything to wear on such short notice."

"Our reservations are for Marikos' Café Alia, so there's no need to get dressed to kill. You can wear that pink silk pants suit you traveled in on our last business trip and we can pretend it's just another day."

"Actually it's peach, but you noticed when I wore it?"

"Apparently." He sounded amused. "You'd probably be surprised at what I notice about you."

"Layton—"

"I'll pick you up at—"

"Layton! I haven't agreed to have dinner with you."

"You will. Won't you?"

He was so sure of himself and her. If only she had half his confidence. She nodded. "Yes."

"I'll see you at six-thirty, honey."

"Okay." She put the phone down and lay on her side, staring at the wall opposite the bed. He was used to getting his way. If they were going to have a child together, she was going to have to stop thinking of him as the CEO to whom she answered and start thinking of him as the father of her child instead.

She needed to learn to assert herself more with him and he would need to learn not to just take her acquiescence for granted.

By six-ten, she was dressed and pacing the length of her living room. None of her attempts to remind herself that she was being silly had been sufficient to dissuade her from the certainly that she was pregnant. Eagerness to see Layton again, warred with confusion and uncertainly how he'd react to the conditions she intended to impose on their relationship.

To help relieve some of her anxiety, she called Benai, who listened in silence. "I have no idea how he'd react, Nai."

"Don't you?"

She sighed. "Okay. I know he won't like my conditions and I know he's used to getting and having his way."

"Aren't you jumping the gun a little, Temp? I mean it's a little early to decide you're pregnant."

"I know this sounds silly but I just feel different. I know I'm pregnant."

"Do you know it or do you just want to be pregnant?"

She sighed. "Okay. I don't know which it is. I just know I'm so nervous."

"I don't think you need to be. Things have a way of working out for people in love."

"Who's in love?"

"Aren't you? Isn't he?"

"Layton? In love with me?" She shook her head. "Now that's wishing for the moon."

"What's wrong with setting your sights high?"

"Nothing…except you have a longer way to fall when your fantasies collapse under you."

"Think positive, Temp. Layton's not self-centered or mean-spirited. If he didn't want more than a one-night stand, he wouldn't have slept with you."

"When? Last night? Today?"

"He wouldn't have slept with you at all."

She nodded. "I know." At least she hoped she did.

"Just take it slowly and expect the best, not the worse from him. If you need to talk, I'm here."

She smiled. "I know. Thanks."

"Relax and enjoy yourself tonight, Temp."

She nodded. "I'll try. 'Night."

"Good night."

She put the phone down and resumed pacing.

Her phone rang just before six-thirty. She stopped pacing and lifted the receiver. "Hello?"

"I'm in the lobby, honey."

She moistened her lips. "Okay. I'll be down in—"

"No. I'll come up for you."

She released the door lock. Five minutes later, the bell outside her apartment door rang. She opened the door. He wore a dark suit with the white shirt opened at the neck. He'd always looked good with a white shirt providing an attractive contrast against his skin tone. She flashed him a quick smile. "Hi."

He stepped inside and leaned against the closed door, smiling at her. "Damn, Tempest. You are one beautiful woman."

She abandoned her tentative plans to keep a buffer between them until they'd had a long talk. Placing her hands against his chest, she tilted her head and smiled up at him. "Talk like that will get you everything you want."

He grinned and slipped his arms around her. "My mama didn't raise any fools, honey, but I mean it."

She nodded. "I know and that's what so amazing."

"Why should my calling you beautiful be amazing when you are beautiful?"

"I've never thought of myself as beautiful, Layton."

"But you are."

She linked her arms around his neck and rubbed her cheek against his. "I like that you think I am." She sighed and stepped away from him. "But before things get out of hand, we need to talk."

He nodded. "Dinner first. Okay?"

"Okay."

"Get your coat and we'll go."

"Okay but I warn you I am not in the mood to listen to any of your somebody done somebody wrong hillbilly music."

He cupped her cheek and stared down at her. "What's the matter, honey? Are you afraid I'm going to do you wrong or are you planning to do me wrong?"

She kissed his palm before pushing his hand away from her cheek. "Neither but you see what listening to that stuff is doing to you? It's making you paranoid."

He laughed. "Okay. I'll allow you to be music director tonight. If I appear paranoid, it's because I'm afraid of losing you."

"I can't imagine your being afraid of anything, Layton."

He frowned. "Then you don't know me as well as you think you do. I'm a normal man with all a normal man's desires and fears. And that wasn't the answer I was hoping for, Tempest."

She met his gaze briefly before looking away. She shrugged. "I know."

"Why are you having such difficulty with this?"

She turned to face him. "It still feels like a dream."

"It's not. It's real."

"I told you I needed a little time to process the change in our relationship, Layton."

"You wanted it to change."

"Yes, I did but wanting something that you don't really think will ever happen and actually having it happen are two very different things. I just need a little time."

"I don't know how patient I can be."

"Try. Please."

"I will but I'm not making any promises."

She nodded.

He sighed. "Let's go before I'm tempted to stay here and try to convince you this is real."

On the drive to Marikos' Café Alia, they listened to soft jazz. Tempest closed her eyes and enjoyed the music and the surprisingly comfortable silence between them.

They were both hungry and kept talk to a minimum as they ate. After the meal, they moved out onto the heated moon room to enjoy the starlit night.

He arched a brow when she ordered decaf but remained silent until their drinks had been bought to their table and they were left alone in their little corner of the room.

He reached across the table and closed a hand over hers. "Are you all right?"

"Yes. Why do you ask?"

"Nothing alcoholic before or with dinner and since when do you drink decaf?"

She shrugged. "I want to be careful."

"Why?"

She resisted the urge to touch her stomach. She'd know soon enough if her suspicions and Brandon's hints were true. "In case I'm pregnant."

His hand tightened briefly around hers. "You think you might be?"

"I'd like to be."

He lifted her hand and brushed his lips against it. "I'd like that too."

A wave of heat washed over her. She tugged at her hand and sat back in her seat. "We need to talk."

He nodded. "Yes, we do, Tempest. I've always wanted to be a father."

"Did you and Allison want kids?"

"Yes."

"What happened then?"

"Nothing. We just didn't want them with each other."

She sucked in a breath. If he didn't want a child with the woman he'd cared enough about to marry, why should she believe he would be a good choice to father her child?

He arched a brow. "What's that look of dismay about? What are you thinking?"

"You didn't want a child with your wife?"

"No and she didn't want one with me. Believe it or not, she and I never had unprotected sex."

"Not even on your honeymoon?"

"Never means never, Tempest."

"I don't understand."

"What's so difficult to understand?"

"You used condoms on your honeymoon?"

"Yes. Look, Tempest, I'm not one of those Neanderthals who thinks sex has to be unprotected to be enjoyable. We both took responsibility to ensure we weren't faced with an unexpected and unwanted pregnancy. I used condoms and she took birth control pills."

"Why didn't you want her to get pregnant?"

"I told you—because we didn't want kids with each other so we made sure she didn't get pregnant."

"That doesn't sound like much of a marriage, Layton."

He shrugged. "It had its moments."

"Were you happy with her?"

"Happy is a relative term. I wasn't unhappy with her…until I met you."

"When you talk like that, you make me feel guilty."

"You have no reason to feel that way."

"When you say you weren't unhappy until you met me, you make me feel almost as if I broke up your marriage."

"You didn't but we were talking about you and the kids I'd love to father for you."

She blinked. "Kids? As in more than one?"

He nodded. "Absolutely more than one."

"How many did you have in mind?"

"Three or four…maybe five."

She bolted forward in her seat. "Five!"

He shrugged. "You know I'm one of nine. A fair sized family is normal for me."

"Yeah, well, I'm an only child and anything more than two or three kids seems…excessive."

"I'll be a good father, honey." He reached across the table and recaptured her hand. "And think of how much we'll enjoy making each and every one of our cherished little treasures."

Her stomach muscles clenched. She licked her lips and eased her hand from his. "We're getting ahead of ourselves. I need you to understand what I'm looking for if we decide to have a relationship."

"If? Tempest, I think it's safe to assume, at least subconsciously, we decided to have a relationship when we made love without protection."

She sighed. "I don't know about you but I wasn't thinking clearly earlier today."

He made an exasperated sound. "How long are you going to continue to make excuses each time we make love?"

His annoyance and brusque tone surprised her. "Come on, Layton. I'm not making excuses. I'm just working my way up to explaining what I need in a relationship."

"Fair enough." He nodded. "I'm listening."

She sipped her decaf before she spoke. "I need to tell you about Brian."

"Your ex-fiancé?"

"Yes. You've probably heard me mention him."

He lowered his lids. "Once or twice. Let's see. You two met when you were both fourteen and fell in love when you were...what? Seventeen? You became engaged at nineteen. You planned to get married after college, wait a few years and then start a family but he was killed in a car accident just after graduation and though you've been involved in at least two semi-serious relationships in the last seven years, you've never fallen in love again." He lifted his lids and met her gaze. "Does that about sum things up?"

She grimaced. "I guess I mentioned him more than once then."

He narrowed his gaze and spoke in a cool voice. "I guess you have."

"More importantly, you really listened."

"Yes. I was interested in the man you considered the love of your life."

She sighed, remembering some of the many good times she and Brian had shared. "He was...Brian was the most wonderful man."

She watched his jaw clench. "So wonderful you've decided you want a child with a man who will allow you to raise his child as Brian's?"

She tensed. "You make it sound unreasonable and...cold or even mean spirited to the biological father."

He gave her a long, silent stare.

"Don't look at me like that. I plan to be completely honest and tell him the truth up front."

"Which is?"

"That I don't want any romantic entanglements, as you called them. I'm not interested in marriage or a serious relationship." She paused and moistened her lips. If that were true, why did she sound so unsure? Why did she want him to object to her spiel? When he didn't, she went on. "And I already have the name picked out."

"And that would be?"

"Brian, if it's a boy and Brianna if it's a girl."

He arched a brow.

She shrugged. "Thanks to my father's real estate investments and life insurance, I'm financially capable of providing for all my child's material and emotional needs alone. I won't expect or require anything from the father of my child once I'm pregnant."

He sat back in his seat. "Charming. So you only need—or should I say want—a man for his sperm."

She blushed. "There's no need to be offensive, Layton."

"What man worth fathering a child with wouldn't find your proposal insulting and offensive?"

She swallowed hard, feeling as if she'd been socked in the stomach. "So you're saying you're not interested?"

"Am I interested in allowing you to disappear into the wild blue yonder with my child? Hell, no, I'm not interested in that arrangement, Tempest!"

Chapter Six

ജ

She stared at him. "If that's how you feel, why did you sleep with me without protection?"

"I've already told you why I made love to you."

She fought to hold back tears. "I don't know where that's going to leave us, Layton."

"Right where we're at now."

"What?"

"Just because I'm not interested in the relationship as you lay it out doesn't mean we can't come to some type of...agreement we can both live with."

She released a sigh of relief. "What did you have in mind?"

"First, you need to understand that I will be involved in my child's life. However, I'm willing to agree that you'd have actual physical custody of our child, providing I have a regular and important part in his life. I understand and accept that you have no desire for a physical relationship after the baby is born and that marriage is out of the question."

For the second time in as many minutes, she felt as if the wind had been knocked out of her. "You do? You accept that?"

He nodded. "Why do you sound and look so surprised? That is what you want of me. Isn't it, Tempest?"

Was it? "I...well, I...that was my plan."

"Then your plan is right on track. Doesn't that please you?"

Hell no! She flashed a cool smile at him.

He studied her face in silence before he spoke again. "If you want something else or your plan changes, you'll have to tell me, Tempest."

"Why am I beginning to feel like a mouse dangling between your paws?"

"I have no idea." He smiled. "Maybe you like being chased and pursued."

"Do you like chasing and pursing your women?

He shook his head. "I only enjoy sex games when my heart isn't involved. If it is, I have to pull out the big guns."

"And what does that entail?"

"You'll know it if it happens between us, Tempest."

"Why can't you just answer my question?"

"Why can't you just trust me not to hurt you?"

"I do trust you!"

"Good. Then you should know I have no intention of shirking any of my responsibilities—including the financial ones."

Her heart raced. "I can live with those conditions."

"I'm glad to hear it," he said dryly. "But there are other conditions on which I won't budge."

Some of her elation evaporated. "And those are?"

"That we maintain our physical relationship during your pregnancy until such time as it becomes unpleasant or painful for you."

She smiled, slowly running her tongue along her lips. "I think I can manage to live with that."

"I'm delighted to hear that, honey."

"What's your other condition or conditions?"

"It's one thing for a little boy to know that his parents aren't in love or committed enough to each other to have been married at some point in time."

She felt a slice of disappointment at his words. Was that his way of warning her not to expect too much from their relationship? Was he telling her he didn't love her and didn't want her love?

He reached across the table to hold her hand. "It's an entirely different proposition for a little girl to know the same thing." He shrugged. "That statement is probably not politically correct, but it's how I feel."

She frowned. "Where are you going with this?"

"I'd want you to have an ultrasound as soon as possible to determine our baby's sex. If it's a boy, fine. If it's a girl I have one more condition."

She'd known him long enough to have an idea where he was headed. Nevertheless, she wanted him to spell it out for her. "If it's a girl?"

He squeezed her hand. "We'll get married."

A surge of joy shot through her. Yes! "Mar…married?"

"Yes. Married, as in come live with me and be my wife and the center of my life."

"The center of your life?"

He nodded.

She blinked. The warm glow turned hot, in a nice way. She struggled not to get lost in a happy haze. He'd married Allison but by his own omission, Allison had not been the center of his life. "But you don't love me, Layton and—"

"You have no idea how I feel—unless I tell you."

And he had *not* said he loved her.

Watching her face, he gave a small shake of his head. "Don't start imagining things, Tempest. I'll tell you what I want you to know about my feelings. For now, let me assure you that no matter what happens, I'll love our daughter and treat you with all the tenderness and respect you deserve."

She stared at him. *What if I want or need more than that from you?*

"I can also promise you that I will not stray. I'll never give you cause to doubt my fidelity, Tempest."

"Layton, I don't know what to say."

"Don't say anything yet. Just listen. I know you don't like country music—"

"But you're going to tell me about a hillbilly song with a message, aren't you?"

He laughed. "Yes, honey, I am."

She smiled. "You have my attention."

"It's by Michael Martin Murphy."

"Never heard of him."

He frowned. "Don't interrupt."

She closed her mouth and made a zipping motion along her lips.

He laughed again. "The song is called 'Long Line of Love'. When the singer meets the one woman he knows is his life mate, he asks her to marry him. Although she agrees, she's not sure their marriage can last. To reassure her, he tells her his grandfather still loves his grandmother and his father still loves his mother. He tells the woman he loves that forever is in his heart and in his blood."

Listening to this, her chest felt constricted.

He went on. "You'll never have to fear that I'm my father's son, Tempest. Like my mother and her mother and grandmother before her, I come from a long line of love. Once we're married, I will never stray."

She was silent for several moments, savoring the thought of being married to him…waking up naked each morning in his arms…having him make love to her on a permanent, regular basis…having him help raise their child…knowing he was there supporting her and their child through the good and the bad times.

She gave herself a mental shake. *Don't get caught up in his sweet, addictive words, girl. For all his talk of his long line of love, he and Allison are divorced. Had he told Allison about his long line of love on his mother's side?* "What if you fell in love with someone else?"

"I wouldn't worry about that if I were you, Tempest."

"Why not? You and Allison—"

"You have my complete attention and interest. I've known a lot of women in my life and I think I can safely promise that you'll have no reason to doubt my...devotion."

"What about Allison?"

"What about her? I never promised her I was devoted to her. I am promising you."

She licked her lips. "Are you saying you feel more for me than you felt for her?"

"Yes."

"Oh."

"And what about you, Tempest?"

"What about me?"

"I think you should know that were you to fall in love with another man, I can promise you that I'd take great delight in kicking his ass all over the city."

She couldn't imagine meeting any man she'd want more than she wanted him. "But you'd let me go?"

His hand tightened around hers. "Sure—but only after hell had frozen over!"

She found his unabashed vehemence exhilarating. "But you divorced Allison."

"She didn't trust me and I didn't love her."

"When did you fall out of love with her?"

He released her hand and sat back in his chair. "I never loved her."

"Never?"

"Never. If I had, she'd have had the devotion I'm promising you."

Devotion was nice but it wasn't love. She parted her lips.

He held up a hand before she could speak. "Before you ask, I married her because I was in big time lust and she had wiles enough to tempt me into marriage. And I'd had my fill of being single. I was tired of one-night stands and a series of meaningless relationships that went nowhere. I wasn't getting any younger."

"What's changed?"

"I'm older and wiser now. I know that marrying for the wrong reason is almost a certain prescription for failure."

"What do you consider the wrong reason?"

"Marrying for any reason other than being in love."

"By that definition, if you and I married, our marriage would be destined to fail."

He shook his head. "I know what I said but you shouldn't count on me ever divorcing you or allowing you to stray. Once you're my wife, you'll be mine forever."

"Forever's a long time."

"With the right woman, it's not nearly long enough."

She stared at him.

He stared back for several moments before he shrugged. "I'm used to getting what I want, Tempest. In case you haven't figured it out by now, I want you as the mother of my kids, as my wife but more importantly, as my life mate."

"Life mate? Is that like wife?"

"For me, a life mate is more than a wife. Wives, unfortunately, sometimes come and go with the wind. A life mate is just what the names implies, a mate for life."

She took a deep breath.

"I'm prepared to do whatever I need to do to win you that way, Tempest."

She flashed him a quick smile. "I want you too, Layton, so you won't have to engage in a hostile takeover to get me."

"Good but if necessary, I can do that too."

"I know."

"Then it's all settled?"

She nodded, a smile spreading across her face. "Yes."

"Yes?"

"Yes!"

"Good." He glanced around. "Would you like to go somewhere to dance?"

Remembering their last dance, she shook her head. "I don't think we're ready to dance together in polite company yet."

He laughed. "Dancing with you does tend to make me lose my heart."

"Your heart?"

"What? Heart? Did I say heart?"

"Yes. You said dancing with me tends to make you lose your heart. Are you saying you're in—"

"I meant head."

"Oh." She felt as if he'd knocked the air out of her lungs. "Did you?"

"Yes. You sound disappointed. Do you want me to be in love with you, Tempest?"

She swallowed slowly, uncertain how to respond. "I don't know now what I want, Layton."

He sighed. "I was afraid you'd say that."

She shrugged. "I know it sounds like a jaded line from a romance novel but this is all so unexpected. Before this morning when I woke up in bed with you, I thought I had my future nicely planned and plotted."

"I assume it didn't include me?"

Her fantasies had. She shook her head. "No."

"And now?"

"And now I'm confused."

"About?"

"Everything…you, me, having a baby with a stranger…having a baby with you—"

He shook his head. "We've already decided that you're having *babies* with me. There isn't going to be any strange men making love to you. You're mine."

Her stomach muscles clenched and she felt breathless. "You sound so certain."

"I am."

"I never agreed to have more than two babies with you."

He smiled. "You will." He lifted her hand to his lips. "You and I are going to spend the next five to eight years making babies we'll both love, adore and cherish."

She stared at him, taking slow, deep breaths. "Oh Layton, when you talk like that, I'm almost ready to agree to anything you want."

He grinned. "That's the plan, honey. I mean to have my wicked way with you as often as possible."

"What if we kept having boys?"

"I'm very fond of boys."

"I couldn't possibly have so many kids as a single mom."

He grinned. "Then isn't it a good thing, we'll be getting married?"

She blew out a breath. "You never asked and I never said I'd—"

He waved a hand. "Whatever. We'll discuss the details later."

"Layton—"

"Yes, I know. I'm being—"

"You're being overbearing and arrogant. And you're assuming I'm going to fall in line with your plans for me."

"Yeah? Isn't that one of the things you like most about me?"

She shook her head but laughed. "Actually, I think it is. I hate to admit it but I do prefer an alpha male."

"There you go. You prefer a man who's prepared to dominate you. Guess what? I'm fully prepared to do just that."

"Hey! Wait a minute! I never said I wanted to be dominated!"

He arched a brow. "But you do. Don't you?"

Her cheeks burned.

"And trust me, honey, I will have my way with you."

"Layton, you —"

He waved a hand. "Never mind denying what we both know is going to happen sooner rather than later. You haven't really touched your coffee. Would you like something else?"

"No. I have a lot to think about and I'm tired. I think I'd like to have an early night."

"Alone?"

Oh how she'd love to spend the night making love with him and then wake up in the morning with his hard, nude body curled against her back. "Yes."

"Why?"

"This is all so sudden and I feel as if I'm being swept off my feet."

"Isn't that what women want from a romantic relationship?"

"Usually but aren't you forgetting something?"

"I don't think so."

"We're not having a romantic relationship."

"Aren't we?"

"No. This is about our both wanting a child without any romantic entanglements."

"So I'm not supposed to romance you? You don't want flowers, presents, cards and dinners out—"

"Of course I want all those things!"

"Then you do want to be romanced?"

"No! Yes!" She shook her head. "I don't know what I want."

"Never mind, honey, we'll figure it out together."

Together. "I like the way together sounds but can we go slowly?"

"That depends what you mean by slowly. If you mean no more making love, then hell no we're not going slowly. After waiting years for the right moment, I'm not going to stop making love to you."

She blushed. "What if I'm already pregnant?"

He shrugged. "Then we'll keep making love as a head start to baby number two."

"You seem to have all the angles figured out."

"I've waited a long time for you, Tempest."

"Oh Layton, when you talk like that you make me feel…" She bit her lip.

"What?"

"I don't know…sexy, beautiful and very special."

"You're all those things, sweetheart. And one more."

"What?"

"Mine. My life mate."

A warm glow spread through her. "I think I'm going to like being yours."

"I know I'm going to like it." He sighed. "Now I'd better take you home before I decide not to allow you to sleep alone tonight."

He was silent on the drive to her apartment. At her door, he cupped one palm over her cheek and kissed the other. "Lunch or dinner tomorrow?"

She leaned close to kiss his cheek. "I'll see you on Monday."

"Are you sure?"

"Yes."

"I could turn alpha and convince you otherwise."

She nodded. "Yes, I know you could but please don't."

"I won't...this time." He turned his head and kissed the corner of her mouth. "Good night."

"Good night, Layton."

Later, thoughts of the previous night spent in Layton's arms kept Tempest awake that night. She shivered with pleasure and lust at the memory and turned onto her side. Slipping her fingers into her pajamas bottoms, she rubbed her pussy, wishing she shared the bed with Layton. She whispered his name and relived their love making of the night before several times before she finally fell asleep.

* * * * *

Tempest woke late Sunday and stumbled into the bathroom. With her thoughts on Layton, she stood under the warm water in the shower stall, rubbing her breasts and fingering her pussy. Her sexual hunger for Layton was shocking and sobering. The thought of having two babies with him and then walking away sent a shudder of dread through her. She wanted him as he'd said he wanted her—forever. To accomplish that, all she had to do was ensure their first baby was female.

And just how do you plan to do that? She sighed. *Just keep your head, girl and be ready to take advantage of all your opportunities.*

The phone rang as she emerged from the bathroom after her shower. Securing the large towel around her damp body, she glanced at the caller id screen, smiled and lifted the phone to her ear. "Hi."

"Hi, honey. I'm downstairs. Buzz me in."

She sank onto the side of her bed. "Layton! What happened to I'll see you Monday?"

"You said that. I just said good night. Consider yourself fortunate I let you sleep alone last night. Buzz me in, honey. I come bearing gifts."

"Gifts? What kind?"

"Buzz me in and find out."

She released the lobby door and rushed over to her closet. She discarded the towel and slipped an oversized nightshirt over her head. She decided there was no point in applying make-up. If she had her way, Layton would just kiss the lipstick off anyway.

Her apartment doorbell rang. She rushed through the apartment to the door. "Who is it?"

"A very horny man bearing gifts."

"A very horny man bearing gifts, huh? My kind of man." She opened the door. "Hi."

He wore a dark waist-length leather jacket open at the neck over a light shirt and dark pants.

As usual, he looked handsome and sexy. He'd look even sexier in a pair of jeans and a cowboy hat.

"You're staring so I'll assume you're happy to see me."

He held a bouquet of roses in his right hand and a large plastic bag in his left hand. She grinned. "Either that or I'm anticipating the gifts you bring."

He feigned a frown. "You're not trying to burst my bubble, are you?"

"Me? Burst your bubble? Never. I was just thinking how great you'd look in a cowboy hat."

"Cowboy hat?"

"Yes. A big, black cowboy hat. Do you have one?"

"No." He bent and kissed her. "I thought you weren't into the hillbilly thing."

"I'm not but you'd look great in a cowboy hat."

"I'll keep that in mind."

"So if I want to see you in one, I guess I'll have to buy it myself."

"I'll think about buying one."

"Good." She urged him inside and leaned against the closed door. "You said something about presents."

"Well, I have roses…" He lifted the bag a few inches. "Breakfast and a present I thought we could share."

"And what's that?"

"My raging lust for you."

She ran her tongue suggestively along her lips. "Yeah? What does this raging lust make you feel like doing?"

"Are you flirting with me?"

"Yes. Yes, I am."

He leered at her. "Really? Do you know what happens to sexy vixens who flirt with horny men?"

She cupped her hands over her breasts. "Why don't you show me?"

He put the food and the roses on the table by the door and slipped his arms around her. "I need to be buried balls deep in that sweet, chocolate pussy of yours." He nibbled at the side of her neck. "Before or after breakfast?"

She slipped a hand between their bodies and cupped her palm over his cock. "Breakfast is so overrated. Let's fuck first."

"I love a woman who has her priorities straight." He swept her off her feet. "Which way to paradise?"

She linked her arms around his neck and stroked her fingers through his hair. "Paradise?"

"Otherwise known as your bedroom."

"That's sweet but the bedroom is too far. Let's do it here."

"Here?" He looked around for a moment before he strolled across the living room to the balcony. On either side of the balcony doors was a set of dark, classic, armless leather chairs Benai had given her as a house warming gift.

He sat her in one. Standing close to her, he kicked off his shoes and then quickly removed his clothes. When he was naked, he pressed her knees apart and pulled her nightshirt off, tossing it on top of the pile of his clothes.

"Okay, honey, you have me naked and horny. What now?"

She reached out and wrapped her fingers around him. "Now I want to eat you."

He caressed her shoulders. "Oh yeah, honey, I love a woman with a plan. Eat away."

"You sit."

They changed places. Once he was seated, she pushed his thighs apart and knelt between his legs. As she gazed up into his dark eyes, she slowly caressed his thighs. She leaned closer, brushing her lips against his chest. The sprinkling of dark hair along his chest tickled her nose. She inhaled deeply, savoring the subtle scent of his cologne.

"I love touching you." She looked in his eyes. "I'm still not sure I can believe I can touch you as much as I like."

"You can touch me as much as you like, Tempest."

She tentatively flicked her tongue against his left nipple.

He made a soft, pleased sound.

She kissed her way across his chest and teased the other nipple.

He repeated the sound and caressed her shoulders.

Encouraged, she rose and sat on his lap, being careful not to make contact with his cock. She settled her lips against his right nipple and reached between his thighs to cup him. As she sucked and licked at his nipple, she gently pumped his dick.

Feeling him swelling against her hand, she licked her way across his chest to his other nipple.

He murmured and cupped one hand over the back of her head. He reached his other hand between their bodies, his fingers probing her slit. "Oh honey...that feels nice...but I'm hard and you're wet."

She bit his nipple and lifted her head to smile at him. "What's your point, handsome?"

"I need you now."

She rubbed her cheek against his. "But I haven't tasted you yet."

"I'm looking forward to that happening-another time. Right now I need to be inside you."

Fully aroused, he pulsed in her hand. She lifted her head, her heart racing and her thighs shaking. Keeping her grip on his shaft, she half rose and then reseated herself—with his cock at her entrance.

He gripped her hips and jerked on them.

She resisted, pushing against his shoulders. "No! I want to feel you going in slowly. I want to enjoy your entrance."

He groaned. "Oh honey, let's have a quick, hard, raunchy fuck first. After we both come, I'll make love to you as slowly as you like."

She caressed his cheek. "Once you're inside, you can thrust all you like...as hard as you like. I just want you to go in very slowly. I just love feeling you inching inside me. It builds my anticipation and makes me want you even more."

"That's my woman."

His woman. It had a nice ring to it. Smiling, she placed both hands on his shoulders again and eased her hips down. The big, warm head of his shaft parted her folds. She closed her eyes and sighed with pleasure when it lodged inside her.

His hands tightened on her hips. "Hey. There's a man under you who needs you with a hunger and passion you can't begin to imagine."

She opened her eyes. "You are so impatient."

"I need you."

His use of the word need instead of want touched an inner hunger in her. "Then take me because I'm yours, all yours," she whispered and sank down onto his lap.

His hard, warm cock plunged up into her.

"Oh!" With her ass on his lap, she linked her arms around his neck. "Satisfied?"

"Hell no!" He shot his cock in and out of her several times in rapid succession before he paused and stared into her eyes. "I won't be satisfied until we both come…and even then the satisfaction will only be transitory."

She rubbed her breasts against his chest. She eased her hips upward, half rising off him. "I want to make you happy. How can I make it last for you?"

"Be mine."

She rocked her hips, shivering with pleasure as his cock moved in and out of her. "I am yours."

"Forever." He jerked her hips down, forcing his shaft back inside her. "Promise me my nights of desire are over. Promise me forever."

"Layton, I—"

He stopped moving in her. "You what?"

They stared at each other in silence.

She felt him almost willing her to bend to his will. She struggled to suppress the desire to obey. "Layton—"

"Just say yes. Promise me forever."

How could she promise that when she wasn't certain he really wanted forever with her? None of his other relationships had lasted more than a few months at most. Why would things be any different with her? She didn't doubt that he meant what he was saying—at the moment. While she'd willingly surrender her body, she wasn't prepared to give her heart for momentary pleasure.

She didn't want to be added to the list of women he'd loved and left.

"I'm waiting, Tempest."

She caressed his cheeks. "I'm yours now, Layton." She wiggled her ass on his lap, eager for sex. Talk about a joint future they might or might not have could come later.

"And that's all you'll promise?"

"Now is all we have. Let it be enough, Layton…until we work things out between us."

"What is there to work out? I'm determined to have you, Tempest. You're my life mate. The sooner you accept that fact the sooner we can get on with our lives."

"If I am your life mate, nothing can change that."

"You are."

"Then you can allow me a little time."

His dark eyes seemed to get darker. His lips compressed.

She almost felt the anger emanating from him. Strangely enough, she knew he would not allow his anger to affect their lovemaking. "Give me a little time, Layton?"

He shook his head. "You've had all the time you're getting."

"I need more, Layton. Just a little more. Please. It's not as if I'm telling you I want to see another man. I just want a little time to process our new relationship."

Without answering, he wrapped his arms around her waist and bounced her up and down on his cock.

The feeling of closeness and rapture she'd felt at the first slide of his cock into her body dissipated some. What was left paled in comparison to the elation she'd felt only moments earlier. Nevertheless, what was left was more than enough when she was more than half in love with him.

She rocked on his lap and rotated her ass wildly, feeling the passion tightening and building in her belly. Tiny embers flickered in her pussy. He shared her desire. She felt it in the tension of his body and in the hard, cock slicing in and out of her. Still, she missed the tender passion they'd shared on Friday night and Saturday morning.

She brushed her lips against his. "Kiss me."

When he failed to obey her soft command, she cupped her hands over his cheeks and pressed her mouth against his. After a moment of resistance, he thrust his tongue between her lips. Devouring her mouth, he took her with a silent fury totally devoid of tenderness. She felt some of his anger seeping into their lovemaking.

The embers turned into a small fire. She increased the movement of her hips, afraid he intended to come before her and leave her aching for fulfillment. Within moments, she knew she'd misjudged him.

With a series of hard, almost brutal movements, he set the small flame in her pussy blazing into a wildfire. Need and desire raced through her body and along her nerve endings, like a fire fed by the Santa Ana winds. Like kindling blown about by the hot, dry infamous winds, she felt totally consumed.

She clung to him and cried out as his pounding hips and hard cock thrust her over the edge of passion and sent her spiraling out of control down into a valley of absolute bliss. His climax followed and less than a minute after her release, he shuddered and pumped his seed into her.

Still holding her tightly, he laid his head on her shoulder.

She held him in silence while her heartbeat returned to normal. Then she kissed his hair. "I just need a little more time, Layton. Please give it to me."

He lifted his head.

Meeting his dark, annoyed gaze, she felt a chill. Not only was he used to getting his way but he was also known for his lack of patience. She feared he wasn't in the mood to be reasonable.

She brushed the back of her hand along his cheek. "I'm only asking for a little time, Layton."

"Asking? You're demanding it. That's not the same as asking."

"Oh Layton, let's discuss it."

"I'm not in the mood to talk, Tempest." He lifted her off his lap and set her on her feet. He turned away from her. "Let's go to bed."

"I don't want to go to bed with you when you're angry with me."

He swung around to face her. "Are you going to ask me to leave?"

"Would you, if I asked you to?"

"Hell, no!"

"Then I won't bother to ask you to go." She bit her lip. "You can have the bed. I'll sleep on the sofa."

He shook his head. "Look, I know you think I'm angry."

"I know you're angry."

"Okay, I am angry but anger isn't my dominant emotion."

"It is from where I'm standing. And I'm not sharing a bed with you in your present mood."

He caressed her cheek. "I've had better moments, Tempest but you won't ever need to be afraid of me."

"I'm not afraid of you."

He sighed and nodded. "Good. Then let's go to bed—together."

"Layton—"

"I'm not leaving and I'm not sleeping alone. So what does that leave?"

She sighed. "I guess we're going to bed together."

"You guess right." He lifted her into his arms.

She slipped her arms around his neck. "One of these days I'm going to challenge you, Layton."

"You go right ahead, Tempest but it's not going to change anything. I always get what I want. And I want you."

"You have me, already."

He shook his head. "I want you on my terms with none of your conditions."

"You can't always have everything you want the way you want it, Layton."

"We'll see. Now let's go to bed."

When she nodded, he carried her to the bedroom.

In bed, she turned to him. "Layton?"

"Yes?"

"Hold me?"

He drew her close, kissing her hair. "For as long as you need me to."

She rubbed her cheek against his shoulder. "And try to be patient with me."

"You know that's not my strong suit, Tempest."

"I know but I need you to dig deep and exercise some for me…with me."

He drew her closer. "I'll try."

"That's all I ask. Just try."

"I'm not making any promises. You know I'm used to getting what I want but I will try."

"Would it hurt just this once if you didn't win?"

"I have to win. If I don't, I lose you."

"You're not going to lose me, Layton. If I'm pregnant, we'll be connected for at least the next twenty or so years."

"That's not what I want and I'm not settling for just being connected."

"We're not going to settle this today."

"No, we're not." He kissed her hair. "Go to sleep. You're going to need your strength for the coming battle—winner takes all."

Knowing she had no desire to win, she smiled and snuggled close to him. He would win. He always got what he wanted but just this once, victory might not be as easy as he hoped. If he had to fight to win her, he'd appreciate her more.

Long after his even breathing signaled that he was asleep, she lay awake. After his unwillingness to even meet her halfway or understand her need for more time, did they even have a future?

He murmured her name in his sleep, his arms tightening around her.

"I'm here," she whispered, kissing his shoulder. She lay listening to his even breathing before she finally slept.

Chapter Seven
ജ

Restless, she woke several hours later. She lay trying to fall back asleep for a while before she slipped out of bed. She picked up the robe on the end of the bed and wrapped it around her body. Moving across the room to her middle bedroom window, she stared out into the dark night of the surrounding woods.

She was ready to return to bed when she heard Layton stirring.

"Tempest? What's wrong?"

She turned to see him sitting up in bed. "Nothing's wrong. I'm just a little restless."

"Why?"

"I...don't know why."

He pushed the covers aside and slipped out of bed. He joined her at the window, embracing her from behind. "What's wrong, honey?"

"Nothing. I just couldn't sleep."

"Why not?"

She shook her head. "I have a lot on my mind."

"Such as?"

"I just want to learn to deal with it for a little while longer."

"It's only a little after two a.m. Come back to bed."

She pressed his hands against her waist. "Is this real?"

"What? Me and you?"

"Yes. Is it?"

He licked the side of her neck. "It's real for me. Doesn't it feel real for you?"

"It feels like..." She turned in his arms and looked up at him. "It feels like one long dream. Before the party sleeping with you was just a fantasy..."

"Was it? Then why weren't you wearing any panties?" He frowned. "Either you were planning to sleep with me or you were planning to sleep with some other man. Which is it?"

She linked her arms around his neck. "I honestly didn't plan on sleeping with anyone—at least not consciously." She smiled. "But after I had a few drinks, you started looking..." She paused and shook her head. "No. I think... I didn't set out to flirt with you on a conscious level but I think I did on an unconscious one." She stroked her fingers through the hair at his nape. "I think I've had an almost subconscious thing for you for a while now."

"Tell me more. How long is a while?"

She shrugged. "Maybe a few years."

His arms tightened around her. "A few years?"

She nodded, reluctant to admit that she had fantasized about him while he was still married.

"Damn! You mean we've wasted years?"

Thank God he hadn't chosen to press her into an admission she wasn't ready to reveal. "I don't think either of us was ready before Friday."

He slapped her ass. "Speak for yourself. I've been ready for about six years now."

"Six years?" She drew away from him. "You were still married then."

"There's no need to look at me like that."

"You said you'd never strayed."

"I didn't."

"But you just admitted—"

"Did I ever give you any reason to suppose I thought of you as anything more than a casual friend while I was married?"

"No but—"

"I meant it when I said I'd never been unfaithful to Allison." He grimaced. "Well…at least, not physically."

"What does that mean?"

"It means I'll admit that emotionally, she's never had my heart."

Had any woman actually ever managed to capture and keep his heart for any meaningful length of time? She was afraid to ask in case he told her no. "Who did she think you were having an affair with?"

"You. Who else?"

"Me? But why would she think that?"

He drew her back into his arms. "She thought she could tell by the way I looked at you. But whatever she thought, I would never have shown you how I felt as long as she and I were still married." He caressed her cheek and tilted up her chin. "I didn't stray with her and I sure as hell will not stray on you."

"So what are you saying?"

"That you have my heart for as long as you want it."

Just how many other women had owned his heart? How many hearts had he broken? If given the chance would he break hers? She doubted her heart would ever be the same if it were broken again. She had recovered from Brian's death but she feared losing Layton would devastate her in a different and even more frightening way.

She wiggled her hips against his. "That's sweet, Layton but right now it's not your heart I'm most interested in."

She saw a hint of annoyance in his gaze before he smiled. "Really? Then what are you interested in?"

"Your cock. I want it and I want you, Layton."

His nostrils flared. "Making love to you is more incredible every time but it's still just sex."

"It's great sex."

"Yes, it is but what if I want more than just great sex?"

She wanted to believe he really did want more but why would he want more than sex with a woman, who was only one skillful make-up session away from being plain? He could have any woman he wanted. Granted he seemed to really want her but if she let her guard down and surrendered her heart to him, what would happen when the novelty of sex with her wore off?

"How much more?"

"A lot more. And what if I want it permanently?"

Her heart raced with joy until she remembered his many supermodel dates. If none of those exquisite women had been able to hold his interest for long, how could she? She'd never known him to date a black woman. Didn't that suggest that she was not his type? "Layton...please...can you just make love to me?"

"Fine. Let's make love."

She reached between their bodies and sighed. "You're not aroused."

"So arouse me."

His voice was cool. She suspected he wasn't interested in making love to her. She didn't want him going through the motions just to please her. "Why don't we do it another time?"

"Are you sure?"

She nodded. She took his hand in hers. "Let's go back to bed."

In bed, he reached for her. "Come here."

She scooted into his arms.

He held her close. "Just so you know, I'm going to get what I want, Tempest. And as you should know, I'll do whatever is necessary to make that happen."

She shivered. She'd seen him ruthlessly crush any business competitor who got in his way. "Layton—"

"Go to sleep and remember in the end, I'm going to win."

"Layton, you're practically promising to hurt me."

"I'm not promising any such thing. You know I would never intentionally hurt you."

Then why did she feel as if the words *unless I have to* hung unspoken in the air between them?

She shivered again, pressing closer to him.

He kissed her forehead and caressed her. He spoke to her in Cherokee until she drifted to sleep.

* * * * *

"You were right." Layton sprawled in his office chair staring out the plate glass windows into the pre-dawn morning.

There was a short silence then a sigh from the speakerphone before Brandon spoke in a sleep-slurred voice. "About?"

"She doesn't love me."

"Are you sure?"

"Yes, I'm sure. Hell, she doesn't even trust me. I know she doesn't love me."

"There's no need for despair, Hawk. I never said she didn't love you."

"If she loved me, she'd trust me."

"A woman can love without trust."

"How?"

"How should I know? I just know they can. Besides, I know she wants to trust you."

"How do you know that?"

"When I touched her, I felt it. I know you're impatient but if you give her a little time—"

"She's had all the time she's getting. I need and want her now. If you're sure she cares…" He allowed his voice to trail off.

"What? What are you planning, Hawk?"

"To make her admit how she feels."

"How are you going to do that?"

"You don't want to know."

"Instead of what you're planning, why don't you just give her the time she needs?"

"I can't wait any longer, Brandon! Can't you understand that? Don't you know how I've suffered for the last six years being so close to her and not being able to tell her how I feel…how much I need her?"

"I know it's been rough, Hawk, but if you rush her—"

"She'll learn to cope. She's very resourceful. I know what she's capable of. That's why we've worked so well together."

"So there's nothing I can say to change your mind?"

"No. Do you know she had the God damned, unmitigated gall to think I'll allow her to name my child after him?"

"Him being?"

"Her damned ex."

"Ex? She's been married?"

"No. She was engaged. He died before they married and she's never forgotten him. In fact she's turned the lucky bastard into a saint and now she wants to worship at his altar. She wants a child she can name after him."

"No shit. What are you going to do?"

"Hell will freeze over before I allow her to name my child after another man. If she's uncertain, I'll give her reason to be—until she's ready to be reasonable."

"Hawk, that doesn't make sense."

"I don't give a shit! I didn't call you to be lectured, Brandon."

"I know and I don't mean to lecture you."

"Then don't! I'm feeling raw and the last thing I need is this."

"I understand that. I just wish you'd reconsider and give her time."

"That's not going to happen. So leave it alone."

"Okay. Fine. I know you're going to do what you think you have to. I'll keep a good thought for you and her, Hawk."

Layton sighed and closed his eyes at the weariness in Brandon's voice. "Listen, I know I woke you, so I'll let you get back to sleep."

"I'm awake now. If you need to talk—"

"You'll be there to listen." He nodded. "I know. You've always been there to listen. And what do you get for it? The nasty edge of my damned temper. I'm sorry."

"For what?"

"I'm the eldest. You should be coming to me for guidance with problems you can't handle alone. I shouldn't be dumping all my emotional baggage on you…especially when you have problems of your own."

"You're two years older, Hawk. That doesn't exactly make you Methuselah but even if you were a lot older, it wouldn't matter. We're brothers by blood and spirit. Even if there were no blood or spirit tie between us, we'd be brothers by choice."

Layton nodded. "Yes. We would."

"Damn right."

"We've had some hard times but I wouldn't trade a single hard time with you and the others for anything."

"We all know that, Hawk. So don't you ever apologize for wanting or needing to talk to me. And don't you ever again call it dumping. You've always been there for us. Each of us from me down to Lelia will always be there for you."

"I know. I'm just feeling like I'm no longer in control of my feelings or emotions."

"I know what you're feeling. It's called being in love."

He nodded. Brandon and to a lesser degree Croft had what their mother had called the gift. They could sense things in others and were nearly always right. "So? How are you?"

"Don't worry about me, Hawk. I'm not quite there yet but I'm dealing with Rissa's death...their death. I won't ever forget but it's getting easier to face life without her. I'm no longer filled with hate and a thirst for revenge. Rissa wouldn't have wanted that."

Layton felt his chest tighten. Sixteen months earlier a paroled convict had broken into Brandon's lover apartment and murdered her. For the first month after her death, Layton and their siblings had stayed with Brandon around the clock, afraid of what his grief and guilt would drive him to do.

Neither Layton nor Bancroft had been able to determine the basis for Brandon's guilt. That in itself was enough to give Layton pause. Brandon usually freely shared his feelings with his siblings.

As far as Layton knew, Brandon had been celibate since Rissa's death. "Are you seeing anyone?"

"No."

"Rissa was a beautiful woman and person. I know you loved her, Brandon but it's time to move on with your life."

"I'm not seeing anyone because I haven't yet met anyone I want to date. When I do, I promise you, I'll date. I'm horny as hell, so count on it." He paused and then went on in an amused voice. "In fact, if you blow it with Tempest, I might steal her from you."

"What?"

"That's quite an ass she has. I'll bet it looks good after a vigorous spanking."

"You'll never know!"

Brandon laughed.

Listening, Layton felt better. The warmth had returned to his laughter. Hopefully he really was on the mend. He yawned. "If you're sure you're all right—"

"I am."

"Then I'm going to shower and dress for work before any of the staff arrives. I'll let you get back to sleep."

"Hawk?"

"I'll be all right, Brandon. I promise."

"Good. Now will you reconsider?"

"No. I have to do what I have to do."

Brandon sighed. "I know. You know I have your back."

"Yes. I do."

"Later, Hawk."

He leaned forward in his seat and released the speakerphone. Then he sank back in his chair. God willing, just this once Brandon would be wrong but at the moment, he was worried about Brandon. He checked his cell phone and then made another call.

"Hello."

He smiled at the sound of one of his younger siblings, Bancroft's voice. "Croft, how's the skiing going?"

"Hawk! How the hell are you?"

"I'm okay. How about you? Are you enjoying the snow and the women in Vale?"

"Both are exciting but I'll be heading back to Pennsylvania soon."

"Why?"

"Well, a friend is leaving for a few months in Paris and she wanted to say goodbye in person."

"Ahhh."

"Yes but I was coming home anyway."

"When are you arriving?"

"Tomorrow morning. What's going on?"

"It's Brandon. I think we really have to do something to help him."

"He's carrying a very heavy load."

"I know and I think he's carried it for as long as he can."

"Declan and I have reached the same conclusion."

"Do you think Declan is up to trying to help him?"

"By himself? No."

Layton rubbed his temple. "I didn't think so."

"Let me clarify that, Hawk. I know Declan is more than willing to try to help him. I just don't think his abilities are strong enough for him to attempt it alone without personal risk to himself."

"I see. Well, I'll have to do what I need to do."

"I know you wear the mantle of your elder status proudly Hawk but don't try to help Brandon alone. As much as we all love him, none of us can help him alone without risking injury to our spirits."

"If anyone has to take the risk, it should be me."

"Hawk—"

"It's all right, Bancroft. It's time to start the healing. I know he loved Rissa but it's time he at least started to date."

"I couldn't agree more. In fact, that's why I'm ending my trip early and coming home."

"You have plans?"

"Not exactly but I've had a very strong…feeling that I need to come home to be in a position to somehow facilitate his meeting someone who may be instrumental in helping him open up and forgive himself."

Layton bolted up in his seat. "Who's this woman?"

Bancroft sighed. "I have no idea. I just woke up from a…dream with the conviction I needed to come home. So I'm coming home and I'll play it by ear when I arrive."

"Is there anything I can do?"

Bancroft sighed. "Since I have no idea who this woman is or how I can get her with Brandon, no. You know these feelings aren't anything I have control over."

But they were nearly always accurate. "Okay. Are you going to need a lift from the airport?"

"No. The lady in question will be picking me up and keeping me busy for the night. I'll see you probably sometime on Thursday."

"Does Brandon know you're coming home?"

"I haven't told him but I'm sure he does. You know he *knows* things. And he's been avoiding me and Declan like we have the plague."

"I see."

"What about you, Hawk? How are you?"

"You've already asked that and—"

"Yes. I know I've already asked that and you said okay but we both know that's stretching things a bit."

"Okay, I'm working on being okay. Is that better?"

"I don't know."

"Leave it for now. I'm not okay but I'm better than Brandon. He's the one we have to help. I'll look forward to seeing you when you return. Have a safe trip, Croft."

"Thanks, Hawk."

* * * * *

When Tempest woke again, she was alone and a dozen roses sat in a vase on her nightstand. She plucked the card from between the roses. "Take the day off, darling."

Darling. While she'd love to stay home, that would make more work for her assistant, who would have work enough in two weeks when she left.

She glanced at the clock and groaned. Eleven fifteen. She was nearly three hours late for work. Layton must have turned off her alarm before he left.

Reaching for her cordless phone, she saw there were two messages from Benai. She sent a text message telling Benai she'd talk to her later. Then tossing the blanket aside, she got out of bed. After a quick shower, she dressed and left her apartment. She stopped at a deli on her way to the office.

Determined not to place an unfair burden on her assistant, she ate her salad at her desk as she worked. She wanted to ensure the department continued to run as smoothly as possible after her departure.

As she worked, she kept expecting Layton to either stop by her office or call her. He did neither. Although surprised, she was too busy to wonder why he didn't make an effort to see her. She lost track of time and was surprised when her assistant tapped on her door to say good night.

"Good night? Already?"

"Yes. It's just after five. Are you working late?"

She shook her head. "No but I'll probably take some work home with me."

"You look tired. Why not go home and relax and start fresh tomorrow?"

She sighed. "That sounds like a good idea. Good night and thanks for covering this morning."

Janice Martin nodded and withdrew from the office.

Tempest sat back against her seat and closed her eyes, allowing her thoughts to turn toward Layton. She'd seen his car in the executive parking area when she'd arrived so she knew he was at work. Why hadn't he stopped by or at least called or emailed her?

She slapped a hand against her head. He'd told her to take the day off. When she arrived home, she'd probably find he'd left at least one message.

Eager to hear his voice, she called her answering machine at home. There were three messages but none of them from Layton. Where the hell was he and why hadn't he called her? She rose and went to look out her office window. She could see the executive parking area. His car, which had been parked two spots from hers, was gone. So he'd known she was at work and had still left without seeing or speaking to her.

Damn him. She returned to her desk and thrust some of the work into her briefcase. Ten minutes later, she left the office. She started her car and drove out of the parking lot.

When Layton showed up at her door later that night, he was going to get a chilly welcome. If she let him in and that was a big if, there would be no sex or "love making" as he insisted on calling their sexcapades.

* * * * *

On the way home, she decided not to sit and wait for Layton to show up. She called Benai from her car, stopped at her favorite pizzeria and drove to Benai's apartment.

Over vegetable stromboli and a garden salad, they discussed the latest best selling thriller they were both reading. Tempest could almost sense Benai's eagerness to ask questions about what had happened between Tempest and Layton after everyone had left the party.

"Thanks, Nai."

"For what?"

"For letting me decide if I want to talk about Layton."

"Do you?"

"Yes and no." She pressed a hand against her forehead.

"Whatever works for you, works for me."

She sipped her ginger ale before she told Benai about the contentious conversation with Layton and spending Sunday night with him. "And now he's avoiding me."

Benai shook her head. "It's too early to assume that, Temp. You said yourself he was a player. He probably needs some time to get back into the one-on-one mode."

She sighed. "That's part of the problem, Nai. I'm not sure he has the will or the desire to really go one-on-one for any real length of time. I've never seen anyone run through women as he's done."

Benai shrugged. "So?"

"So?"

"Yes. So? First you didn't think he was interested. Now you think he's avoiding you. Just maybe he's had a lot of lovers because he'd been waiting for the right one to come along." She grinned and pointed a finger at Tempest. "That would be you, you lucky girl! I can only imagine what it's like to have a big, sexy hunk like him in hot pursuit." She gave a gusty sigh. "You get to live it. So do me a favor. Okay? Stop worrying and enjoy it enough for us both."

Tempest's smile vanished. She and Benai had been friends since junior high. During that time, she and Benai had often discussed their lack of beauty. Benai's favorite refrain had been, "Yeah but you only think you're plain. I actually am."

While she knew Benai was not beautiful in the traditional sense, she had a beautiful smile, a great personality, a passionate, giving disposition and she was intelligent. "Don't get maudlin, Nai. You have a lot to offer a discerning man."

She nodded, her dark brown eyes sparkling with amusement. "I couldn't agree more. I just have to find a hunky man who agrees with us."

"It'll happen for you. I just know it will. If I can attract Layton, even if it's only temporarily, there's no reason why you can't attract a hunk of your own. Just don't give up."

Benai smiled. "I won't but I'm a realist. I know I'll meet my soul mate and get married one of these days. I know we'll be very happy. But I know he won't look anything like your Layton." Her smile turned into a grin. "More's the pity."

Tempest sipped her ginger ale. "But is he my Layton? And if he really is, how long will it last?"

"I'll bet it will last as long as you want it to. So don't jump to conclusions. Okay?"

She nodded. "You're right. I'm probably over reacting."

"Why do you doubt his word?"

"I don't. It's just that I know what type of women he likes to date and I don't fit the mold."

"Maybe not but you clearly rocked his world."

"I know and I'd feel more confident if he hadn't had so many lovers and if he weren't so damned…oh, what word do I want?"

Benai leered. "Hunky? Gorgeous? Delicious? Choose your poison."

"Actually, he's all those things and more."

Benai licked her lips in an exaggerated fashion. "All the more reason to give him a little room and time to fall even harder for you."

"Don't I wish?"

"Don't wish, Tempest. Make it happen."

She nodded. Maybe she would…if the damned hunk stopped avoiding her. She glanced at her watch. "I'd better get home." *In case he comes or calls and I'm not there.*

Benai nodded silently, an understanding look in her dark eyes.

Two and a half hours later Tempest lay sleepless in bed. Where the hell was Layton? Her anger had dissipated over the course of the evening. If he called, he'd get a much warmer welcome than she'd planned on giving him earlier.

Around eleven thirty, she got out of bed with the intention of calling him. She dialed his cell phone but hung up before the first ring. She was not going to chase him. She'd done that at his party. That hadn't worked out very well for her.

She took a short soak in the tub and got back in bed. A little after twelve, she fell asleep. She woke several times during the night longing for him. At some point, she realized that, if she were pregnant, she wanted a boy she could name Layton. She experienced a moment when she felt disloyal to Brian's memory. She shook it off. Brian had loved her and would have wanted her to be happy.

Her chances of being happy with Layton didn't look promising. Nevertheless, she at least wanted a chance to try with him.

Chapter Eight

ಬ

In the morning, Tempest felt tired and irritable. As she showered, she noticed that her breasts were sore. She groaned. The way her luck was running, she was almost certainly pregnant. Now that she was, Layton was obviously having second thoughts. He would get cold feet just when she was ready to tell him regardless of the sex of their baby, she wanted to marry him.

His car wasn't in the executive parking area when she arrived at work. She frowned. He was rarely late for work. Where the hell was he? Who the hell was he with? She'd been a fool to believe all his protestation of her having his full attention and his never straying. Why would a man who could have any woman he desired settle for one? He probably wouldn't recognize forever if he tripped over it.

She ate breakfast at her desk as she worked. Several hours later, she got up and looked out into the parking lot. Layton's car was there. Damn him! If he thought he was going to brush her off after getting what he wanted, he was sadly mistaken.

She stalked from her office and walked down the hall to the executive offices.

His secretary, Barbara smiled as Tempest paused by her desk. "Good morning, Ms. Marshall."

"Good morning, Barbara. Is Layton in?"

"He's in a meeting in the third floor conference room."

"Do you know how long he'll be?"

"No, I don't. Would you like me to ask him to call you when he's free?"

So he'd know she was running after him again? "No, thanks. I'm sure I'll see him around some time today. I'll talk to him then."

The day passed without her encountering him. At five o'clock, she glanced out her office window. Layton's parking space was empty. He was definitely avoiding her! What was she going to do about it? She caressed her stomach. Her period was due in less than ten days. If she got it, the chances of her being pregnant would be practically nil. She could leave the company and never have to see Layton again. As things stood now, if she were pregnant, things were going to be very uncomfortable between them.

After another restless night, she reluctantly went to work on Wednesday. Layton's car was not in his space. She sighed and entered the building. She spent nearly an hour trying to concentrate on work before she picked up the phone and called Benai.

"I need a pick-me-up. How about dinner out tonight?"

Benai sighed. "You haven't seen or heard from him yet?"

"No." She paused, remembering his promise to do whatever was necessary to get his way. "He plays hardball and he plays to win. He's probably going to try and wait me out."

"Wait you out?" Benai sounded confused.

"Because he didn't get what he wanted, he'll probably make me chase after him. He probably won't be satisfied until I...humiliate myself to get him back."

"Tempest...if you think that, he's not a very nice man."

"Don't misunderstand me, Nai. He is a good man. He's very generous with his time and his money. He does volunteer work and he donates more to charity than some people think he should."

She nodded. "I know what he donates but how do you?"

"About six years ago, when he was still married, we were going on a business trip. It was my turn to pick him up. When

I arrived at his house, I drove around the side. The patio doors were open and I could hear Allison yelling at him that she was tired of him giving their money away. I couldn't hear his response but she went on to name a list of luxury items they could have bought with the money he'd donated to charity that year."

"She sounds like she was quite the selfish gold digger."

"I'm not saying she was a gold digger."

"Sure sounds like she was. I mean she didn't even work while they were married, they didn't exactly live on skid row and she always looked as if she'd just finished shopping at the most expensive boutique she could find. He treated her well."

Tempest shrugged. "He gave her lots of material things."

"It sounds like that's all she deserved—material things. Maybe they deserved each other."

"Oh no. He's a good man. He's just used to having his way."

"It's one thing to be cutthroat in business but in love?"

"Who said anything about his being in love?"

"Are you in love?"

"Probably."

"Probably? Oh Temp, are you forgetting who you're talking to?"

"Okay. I am. Satisfied?"

"I will be when you give him what he wants."

"Why should I?"

"Because you love him. Isn't that reason enough?"

She sighed. "Maybe…if he loved me."

"Oh Temp, come on. If he didn't love you, why would he want you to promise to be his forever?"

"I don't know!" She compressed her lips. "But I'm sure I'm not the first woman he's asked that of."

"So? What matters is that you make sure you're the last one he wants it from."

"If I could just be sure that was probable, I'd gladly go chasing after him."

"Temp—"

She shook her head. "This is not the time for this conversation. Can you make dinner tonight at Joni's?"

"Yes. Do you have reservations?"

"No but Layton has two standing reservations there for Wednesday nights. We can use those."

"You're sure he won't be using them?"

"Since he hasn't asked me to dinner tonight, he'd sure as hell better not be using them."

"Great. I'll see you at seven."

"Let's make it six. I want to make a quick stop at the western shop at the mall."

"The western shop? Do I want to ask why?"

"I'm in the market for a big, black cowboy hat."

"Hmmm. Okay. Six it is."

Tempest hung up and sat back in her chair. She closed her eyes briefly, then gave herself a mental shake. She needed to prepare for her last staff meeting that afternoon. That didn't leave any time to waste feeling sorry for herself. Besides, things would work out between her and Layton—even if she had to chase him.

* * * * *

Layton sat in his office staring out his office window. Several times that day, he had been tempted to walk down the hall to Tempest's office, go down on bended knee and beg her to marry him. But he was determined that would not happen until after she was ready to agree to a long-term commitment with him. While he was fairly confident she felt more than just

117

desire or lust for him, he wanted more. After waiting so long for her, he doubted that he could be satisfied with anything less than her unconditional love and promise of eternal fidelity.

And if he had to avoid her to get her to that point, so be it. He could not afford to waiver. He had to hold out and force her to admit she loved him as much as he loved her. Once she did that, she should be willing to admit she was his woman forever. If she were in half as bad a shape as he was, she'd come to her senses very soon. He hoped.

He closed his eyes and sighed. Damn it was so difficult staying away from her. *But you have to. So deal with it.*

His private line rang. He sat forward and picked up the receiver. "Hello."

"Hello, Layton."

He sat back in his chair. "Cheryl. This is a surprise."

"I hope it's a nice one, Layton."

Damn. He didn't need this. "How are you?"

"Lonely. Are you free for dinner?"

"No. I'm not."

"Can I buy you a drink?"

"Thanks but—"

"What? Let me guess. You've replaced me already."

He'd ended their relationship because he'd suspected she was starting to feel more for him than he wanted her to. "If you're asking if I'm seeing someone else, then yes, I am."

"Who is she? Anyone I know?"

"Cheryl—"

"Is it serious? If it's not, maybe we could—"

"No. We couldn't."

"Why not?"

"The days when I thought it was fun to date more than one woman at a time are long gone."

"So…it's really over between us."

"Yes."

"Are you sure, Layton? Because—"

"I'm very sure." He raked a hand through his hair. "If I did anything to hurt you, I'm sorry. I never intended that."

She laughed. "Not everyone can turn off their feelings as easily as you apparently can, Layton. For some people…sex is special and—"

Damn! He clenched his jaw before he spoke. "And I was very clear from the start what I did and didn't want from our relationship, Cheryl. I never lied to you."

"And that made it easier for you to just toss me aside when you'd had enough? Tell me, Layton, are you going to use your new lover as a wind up sex toy too?"

He didn't respond.

"Well…I guess I should hang up before I really embarrass myself."

"Goodbye, Cheryl."

"Fuck you, you cold, selfish bastard!" She slammed the receiver down.

Another angry ex-lover. Why the hell couldn't some women just let go when a relationship was over? He put the phone down and closed his eyes. He was getting too damned old to deal with this shit. God, willing, Cheryl would be the last disgruntled ex he'd have to deal with.

* * * * *

Later that night, after an hour spent at the western shop in the mall, Tempest and Benai picked at their dessert over dinner.

"You want to talk about him?"

Tempest shook her head and placed her fork next to her plate. "No. I just didn't want to spend the night alone waiting for him to call."

Benai frowned. "Say what, girl? You mean we're not having dinner out because of my sparkling personality and charming wit?"

Tempest laughed. "Of course we are." She picked up her fork again.

Benai nodded. "I thought as much. Hmmm."

Tempest looked up to see Benai was looking past her. "What?"

Benai looked at her. "There's a hunk looking this way...staring at you. For a moment, I thought it was Layton but it's not him. This hunk is with a supermodel type. He...oh...he's headed this way."

Tempest turned. A tall, handsome male with dark eyes and almost black hair pulled back in a ponytail strolled toward their table.

She smiled and extended her hand. "Bancroft!"

Brandon's twin paused at the table. "You're looking lovelier than ever, Tempest." He took her hand in his and bent to press a warm kiss against her cheek.

Tempest looked behind him. "Are you here alone?"

"No. My date has gone to powder her nose." Still holding Tempest's hand, he turned to look at Benai. "Introduce us, Tempest."

Tempest glanced up and noted he was staring at Benai. She sucked in an excited breath. "This is Benai Peters. Benai, this is Bancroft Grayhawk."

Bancroft released Tempest's hand and moved around the table to take Benai's hand in his. "Benai. What a lovely name."

As Tempest watched in surprise, Bancroft lifted Benai's hand and pressed a quick kiss against the back.

Benai smiled. "It's nice to meet you."

"Oh believe me, Benai, the pleasure is all mine."

Benai grinned. "Oh...well...I'm sure it is."

"You have the most beautiful color skin I've ever seen, and your smile..." He smiled. "You are absolutely perfect but I'm sure you've heard that before."

Benai blinked at him, her dark eyes wide. Then she pulled her hand from his and sat back in her seat. "Sure. I hear it all the time."

He nodded, still staring at her. "Damn." He glanced at her left hand. "You're not wearing a wedding ring."

Benai nodded. "Yes. I noticed that."

"So did I."

"Ah...shouldn't you get back to your date?"

Tempest heard the sudden coldness in Benai's voice and sighed. Benai didn't believe him. Tempest could fully understand Benai's disbelief. She herself had difficulty accepting that Layton could possibly be romantically interested in her.

Bancroft sighed. "I see you're misunderstanding me." He glanced over his shoulder. "But you're right. I should get back to my date. She doesn't like to be kept waiting."

"I'm sure she doesn't."

"But we'll see each other again, Benai. When we do, I'll explain." He turned to smile at Tempest. "Hawk's a lucky man." He cast a quick look at Benai. "And Hawk's going to be one as well...unless I decide to let him find his own woman."

Tempest cast a brief, uncertain smile at him. She knew Layton was called Hawk by his younger siblings and Bancroft clearly knew of the change in her relationship with Layton. But she had no idea what he'd meant by his remark as he looked at Benai. He'd discover soon enough that she and Layton were far from a real couple.

"Have a good evening, ladies." He turned to smile at Benai again before he returned to his own table.

Benai frowned at her. "What was that all about?"

Tempest shook her head. "I have no idea but I hope he didn't creep you out."

Benai shook her head. "No. He probably should have but he didn't. I'd just like to know what he was going on about. Clearly he wasn't serious."

"Why not?"

"Since when am I absolutely perfect? What am I supposed to be perfect for? Clearly not for dating him."

"Why not for dating him?"

"Why not?" Benai arched a brow. "Look, Temp, I know you're my cheering section and I appreciate it."

"But?"

"But there is no way a man who looks like him would be interested in dating me."

"Why not? Layton wants to date me."

Benai cast a quick gaze ceiling ward. "You may not be the next Miss America but you are not plain. We both know that I am."

Tempest parted her lips.

Benai held up a hand. "And before you go on about my *amazing* smile and gorgeous body, let's remember men want a face to go with those things. Besides, you can see what kind of woman he's with."

"So? Layton dated the same type but that didn't stop him from practically consuming me when we were alone. Maybe, like most people, they like trophy dates but when they're ready to get serious, they go for things that are more important and more lasting than mere physical beauty."

"Don't I wish?" Benai waved a hand in dismissal. "But let's not talk about him anymore."

"Okay but just let me say this. I don't know Bancroft well but I don't think he'd deliberately mislead you about his interest."

"Really? Bancroft is an honorable man but Layton isn't? He'd mislead you about his interest but Bancroft wouldn't mislead me?"

Tempest sighed. "No. I don't think Layton would do it intentionally. No."

"I'll tell you what, why don't we both give them the benefit of the doubt?"

Tempest shrugged. "I'm trying to do that but so far he hasn't made any attempt to contact me."

"So you contact him."

"No. If he really cares, he'll call me."

Ben grimaced. "Be reasonable, Tempest!"

"I'm trying but it's not easy."

"Why not?"

She swallowed hard and spoke in a soft voice. "Because I'm in love with him"

"Have you told him?"

"No. I'm only now getting to the point where I've admitted it to myself…and you."

"You should tell him, Temp, it might make all the difference."

"It won't—unless he loves me too," she said.

"You won't know that until you give yourself a chance to find out how he feels."

She nodded. "I will—when he contacts me."

"Oh Temp!"

"I need him to want me enough to go out of his way and do something different just to get me. Is that too much to ask?"

"You should ask him that," she responded.

"I would—if I weren't afraid of the answer."

"I can understand how you feel but sometimes in order to get what you want and need from a relationship, you have to take some risks."

"If I could just be sure—"

"If you were sure of how he feels, there wouldn't be any risk involved."

She sighed. "You're right. "

"And?"

"And we'll work it out between us."

"When?"

She smiled. "As soon as he gives in."

Benai rolled her eyes. "You are impossible, girl."

She laughed. "Maybe so, but Layton thinks I'm beautiful."

"I know he does."

* * * * *

Later that night, as Tempest lay in a bubble bath, the phone rang. She sat up and picked up the cordless phone, which lay on the floor beside the tub. She glanced at the ID. Noting an unfamiliar number, she frowned, before deciding to answer. "Hello?"

"Tempest?"

"Yes." She hesitated. "Bancroft?"

"Yes." He sounded pleased at her recognition of his voice.

"This is a surprise."

"If you're wondering how I got your number, Hawk gave it to me."

He could give out her unlisted number without her permission but couldn't bend enough to meet her half way. Damn him. If he just bent a little, she'd bend too and then they could—

"Tempest?"

She blinked and shook her head. "Sorry. What were you saying?"

"I wanted to ask you about Benai."

A pleased smile spread across her face. So he *was* interested in Benai. Yes! "What about her?"

"I noticed that she didn't wear a ring. Is she married or in a committed relationship?"

Recalling Benai's lack of enthusiasm at Bancroft's interest, Tempest struggled to contain her glee on her friend's behalf. "Why do you ask?"

"Isn't it clear?"

"Yes but frankly, I didn't think she was your type."

"Actually, I'm not aware that I have a particular type. I like to think I'm mature enough to realize that women worth dating come in all sizes, colors, shapes and even with varying degrees of attractiveness. A woman doesn't have to be a traditional beauty to catch my interest."

Tempest listened in silence, impressed. Benai was going to be in for a nice surprise when she learned what depth Bancroft possessed.

"However, I'm not inquiring about her for myself. More's the pity."

Tempest compressed her lips. "Then who are you asking for?"

"Hawk. I think she would be perfect for Hawk. What do you think? She's your friend. Do you think she'd be interested in him?"

Tempest gasped and nearly dropped the receiver. "Hawk?"

"Yes. Do you think he's her type?"

"No! What kind of friend do you think she is? She would never go out with him!"

"Why not? Does she only date black men?"

"She doesn't date her best friend's lover no manner what color they are!"

"Her best friend's lover? You and Hawk? Oh my God, Tempest. How could you do this to him?"

He sounded so shocked and angry, Tempest sucked in a quick breath. She must have misunderstood him. "How could I do what to who?"

"Sleep with Hawk!"

"I thought you knew. Didn't Brandon tell you?"

"If he had, he'd have been knocked on his ass the minute he had."

She frowned. "Why should my having slept with Layton bother you so much? I thought you — "

"Layton? You meant you and Layton are lovers?" She heard the relief in his voice.

"I hadn't planned on announcing it to your entire family but never mind that now. Who did you think I meant when I said Benai wouldn't date her best friend's lover?"

"Hawk."

Tempest frowned. "She wouldn't date Layton!"

"I don't mean Layton."

"You said Hawk, Bancroft!"

There was a moment of silence and then she heard his rich, deep laughter. Her nostrils flared. "What's so funny?"

"Forgive me, Tempest. Obviously Hawk hasn't told you of our little family custom."

She blinked. "What custom?" With her luck, she was about to be told the Grayhawk brothers bedded each other's lovers.

"In our family the eldest male siblings are called Hawk."

"And that would be Layton."

"I said siblings, Tempest. Layton is Hawk to us all but as the next eldest, Brandon is also Hawk to those of us younger than him. In turn, I am also called Hawk by the siblings younger than me."

"What? Layton, you and Brandon are all called Hawk? What happens when you're all together?"

"We're still all called Hawk."

"Then how in the world do you know which Hawk is which?"

He laughed again. "As you'll learn, we're a very close family with ties that most people wouldn't understand or share within their family. When we're together, we know which Hawk is being referred to."

"Lovely." She moistened her lips. "So when you asked if Benai was interested in Hawk, you meant Brandon?"

"Of course. I think we all know Layton belongs to you."

Now if she only shared his certainty. "Oh." She sighed in relief.

"So is Benai committed to anyone?"

"No, but as far as I know she and Brandon have never met."

"They haven't but I plan to rectify that."

"What makes you think Brandon will be interested in her?"

"She'll be as good for him as you are for Hawk."

She hesitated. "I don't know how to tell you this, Bancroft but Layton and I aren't exactly getting on like a house on fire at the moment."

"You will."

"You sound so certain."

"I am."

"Why?"

"You're his life mate. Sometimes life mates have rocky starts but everything works out in the end because they are meant to be together."

"What makes you think we're meant to be together?"

"He told us all several years ago. Why do you think we've all gone out of our way to see you as often as possible? We all knew it was only a matter of time before you and Hawk got together."

Got together. Not married. Oh hell, the way things were going for her at the moment, getting together with Layton would be the best she could hope for. It would be enough. "I see."

"So about Benai. Can I make arrangements to have her and Hawk meet?"

"Can you do me a favor?"

"Of course. Name it."

"Please call him Brandon when you're talking about fixing him up with another woman."

He laughed. "I'll do my best. Now, about Benai—"

"We both thought you were interested in her yourself…or at least I thought you were."

He sighed. "She has the most beautiful chocolate skin I've ever seen and that smile of hers…hell, if Brandon isn't interested, I sure as hell would be. Do you think she'd go out with either or us? Or even both of us?"

"Both? Bancroft!"

"That way she could decide which of us she preferred."

"Do you and Brandon…date the same women at the same time?"

"Why don't you ask what you really want to know?"

"Which is what, wise guy?"

"If we sleep with the same women at the same time."

"Do you?"

"All you really need to know is that Layton doesn't. He's a one woman man and you're his one woman."

"Nice try, Bancroft but we're talking about you and Brandon."

"We're identical twins. We often share things."

"Does that include women?"

"Would Benai object if it did?"

"Would she object? What kind..." Tempest trailed off, suddenly aware that she had no idea if Benai would object.

"Honey? I'm cold and horny. Come fuck me and warm me up."

Tempest heard a muzzled response and assumed Bancroft had placed his palm over the receiver. She rolled her eyes. He was trying to make a date with Benai while his current lover wanted him in her bed? His lack of fidelity didn't bode well for any possible relationship between him and Benai. Did Brandon share his twin's lack of values?

"You sound like you already have your hands full, Bancroft."

"This is nothing of consequence."

Charming. Did all the Grayhawk men sleep around like Bancroft and Layton apparently did?

As if he knew what she was thinking, he went on. "Marla and I are friends with benefits but only friends. She's on her way to Paris for several months and wanted to say goodbye. Neither of our hearts is involved and I'm not proposing to cheat on her with Benai. If you like, I'll put her on the phone and you can ask her yourself."

She believed him. She sighed, not sure she should. "Thanks but that's not necessary. Maybe we'd better continue this conversation later. I'll talk to Benai and get back to you. Where are you staying?"

"With Hawk, where else?"

"Hmmm. Which Hawk would that be?"

"Layton."

"Oh…then maybe you'd better call me in a few days."

"Why?"

"I don't want to talk to Layton…unless he calls me." She bit her lip. What was it about Layton's brothers that made her comfortable telling them things she ordinarily wouldn't?

"Don't be like that, honey. I'll wait for your call at Ha— Layton's place. 'Night."

"Good night."

Chapter Nine

✍

She ended the call and quickly finished her bath. After drying off and slipping on a nightshirt, she got in bed. Reclining against her pillows, she called Benai, who listened in silence as she spoke.

"What do you think, Nai?"

"What do I think? About which one of them?"

"Either one of them. They're both handsome men. Does the possibility of their both wanting to date you turn you off?"

Benai laughed. "Why in the world would I be turned off by two handsome men who might want to take me out? That's more like a fantasy than a nightmare any day."

"Oh. Great. Can I give Bancroft the go ahead?"

"No."

"Why not?"

"I'm not convinced it wouldn't be a waste of all our times. I saw the woman he was with. She was drop-dead gorgeous. If that's his type of woman, he's not likely to be interested in me."

"Oh Nai—"

"Besides, I'd just assumed we got you and Layton squared away before we start worrying about me."

"Oh Nai, that's sweet but you shouldn't put your love life on hold on my account."

Benai laughed. "Get a grip, Temp. I'm not putting anything on hold. Brandon and I haven't even met."

"You've met Bancroft."

"Yes. I have. Temp, do you really think he was serious?"

"Yes. I do."

"Wow."

"So what shall I tell him?"

"For now? Nothing. What you and Layton share is worth fighting for. Let's do you and Layton first. Then we'll chase those handsome, long-haired, hunky brothers of his for me…maybe."

"Which one?"

"Maybe both of them."

"Nai! Really?"

"Oh come on, Temp. Why do you sound so shocked? Surely you've fantasized about taking on two men at once?"

"Yes but both men were always Layton."

"Well, didn't you say Bancroft and Brandon were identical twins?"

"Yes."

"So there you go."

"Then why not let me tell Bancroft—"

"No. You first. Then me. Okay?"

"Nai—"

"It will be an incentive for you to bend a little."

"You're impossible, Benai."

"Yes, Temp, I know but you love me anyway."

"Yes. I do."

"Now take your butt to bed and sleep on that pride of yours."

"I will—you pain."

She hung up on the sound of Benai's laughter.

* * * * *

The following night, Layton was working out some of his mounting sexual frustration in the basement gym of his mansion when Brandon walked in. Layton continued with his leg presses.

"Have you talked to Tempest lately?"

"No."

Brandon sat on the adjacent bench "Are you planning to call her?"

"No."

"What if she calls you?"

"Then I'll know I'm not in love alone anymore."

"And what if she's thinking the same thing and is waiting and hoping you'll call?"

Layton sat up and straddled the bench. "She's the one who didn't want to commit to anything more than the moment. It's her move."

Brandon nodded. "And you're okay?"

"I'm fine."

"You are?"

"Yes!" he snapped, annoyed at Brandon's persistence.

Brandon reached out to touch his shoulder. Layton jerked back and closed his hand around Brandon's wrist. They stared at each other in silence. After several moments, Layton sighed and released Brandon's hand. "Okay. Fine. I'm not fine. Satisfied?"

Instead of the probing touch that Layton sometimes found invasive when he didn't want his deepest emotions exposed, Brandon clasped his shoulder. "It's okay to allow the woman you love to wrap you around her finger. Believe me. Let her have her way, Layton. Being stubborn and insisting she yield to you is counterproductive. And if something happened to her and you never got a chance to—"

He gripped Brandon's shoulder. "Something happen to her? Have you seen or felt something?" He resisted the urge to shake Brandon. "Tell me!"

"No but I'm thinking of the mistake I made with Rissa, a mistake I'd finally intended to rectify but never got the chance. Don't make a mistake with Tempest you may not get the chance to fix."

Sensing Brandon might finally be ready to share his pain, Layton suppressed the urge to continue pressing him about Tempest. "What happened?"

"I…she never really asked for much and she trusted me from the moment we met." Brandon sighed. "She was a virgin when we met. Imagine that. A twenty-five-year-old virgin — in this day and age."

"Amazing."

Brandon nodded. "She was amazing in many ways. She was beautiful, sexy, innocent and so very trusting. I knew I had to have her the moment I saw her. God, she was so beautiful with all that long, dark brown hair and those amazing green eyes. All she wanted was to be married before she got pregnant."

Layton sighed. That clearly had not happened. He remained silent and waited for Brandon to continue.

"I knew she was in love with me within weeks of our meeting and I used that knowledge against her. She didn't want to sleep with me but I pressured her into it because I wanted her so much. And then I was a selfish bastard and didn't use protection. I was hell-bent on coming in her. Well I did and she got pregnant almost immediately. Then, double dumb-ass, self-centered bastard that I was, I wouldn't marry her. I knew she needed to know I wanted to marry her. But because I didn't believe in marriage, I held out. By the time I changed my mind…it was too damned late. I never got a chance to prove my love to her. I had the ring in my pocket when I…found her."

The pain in Brandon's eyes generated a tightness in Layton's chest. "We all make mistakes, Brandon. So you made one. You were going to make it right. You can't keep beating yourself up over a mistake."

Brandon looked up. The guilt Layton saw in his gaze made him ache. He sucked in a breath. "It's over, Brandon. Forgive yourself."

"I'm trying. I am. I'm working on it. Please, Hawk, don't make a mistake with Tempest you might not have time to make right."

"I hear you and I understand. I just need... I'll... I have to... Things will work out okay between us, Brandon. Don't worry. Just concentrate on healing. Tempest and I will be fine."

"She's pregnant, Hawk. She needs to know she can depend on you."

He stiffened. "She knows that."

"How can she if you won't even call her?"

"I need her to give me a sign. If she does, I'll walk barefoot over hot coals to make her happy."

"I can't imagine that she's very happy at the moment."

"Neither am I."

"I know but you're not pregnant by a man who won't talk to you unless you make the first move."

He raked a hand through his hair. "You're making me sound unreasonable."

"You are being unreasonable."

"I don't want a lecture, Brandon."

"You might not want one but you need one."

"Look—"

"Is this really the way you want to treat your *sheenea*?"

Layton narrowed his gaze. Although he had loved and respected his mother, he was a modern, practical man. Even while acknowledging that Brandon and Bancroft had abilities most people did not possess and their brother Declan seemed to have the ability to help others heal, Layton hadn't always understood her beliefs in some of the ancient tales and lores.

She had firmly believed that their father, Joseph, had been her *sheenea*, the one person in the universe who completed her and made her who she was. When he had strayed, she had lost part of herself and never recovered it. Her belief in that ancient lore had eventually killed her as she'd lost her will to live. Damn if he would allow that to happen to him.

"I never said Tempest was anything but a woman I love."

"Are you going to tell me you don't belief she's your life mate?"

"Yes but that doesn't mean—"

"You know the term life mate is derived from *sheenea*."

"I know that's what you, mother, Bancroft and probably Declan believe."

"We all believe it, Hawk, even you and Randall, if you two will only admit it. We all believe it because it's an integral part of who we all are. That's why you're afraid of allowing Tempest to draw you to her—because you know she's your *sheenea*. You know you can't ever be complete without her. And you're afraid of the power that truth would give her over your heart and happiness."

He sucked in a deep, aching breath. "Don't preach to me, Brandon! And don't tell me what I believe or what I'm afraid of! Tempest is my life mate. I never said I believed in *sheenea*."

"But you do. We all do. It's the basis for our long line of love concept. Sometimes there's only one true *sheenea* and if we don't embrace and celebrate her while we can, we may be destined to be hungry for love forever. There is no forever or long line of love without one's *sheenea* by one's side."

He stared at Brandon. "Don't say that, Brandon."

"We both know it's true, Hawk."

He clenched a hand into a fist. "If it is, where the hell does that leave you without Rissa?"

Before Brandon glanced away, Layton saw a bleak look in his brother's eyes that sent a chill of fear through him. "Brandon?"

Brandon shook his head. "I don't know, Hawk. I just know you can't afford to make the same mistake I did."

Layton could feel Brandon's pain and anguish hanging between them. In that moment, he feared for Brandon having lost the one person he felt completed him. He had watched as a similar belief had slowly killed their mother, sapping her strength until there had been no will to live in her—even for the sake of the many children who loved and honored her.

He didn't possess any of the ancient abilities many of his siblings did, so he had to help in the only way he could. He extended his hand. "Give it to me."

Brandon shook his head. "No. It's too much, Hawk. I can barely contain it."

"Give it to me."

"No! Why do you think I've avoided Croft and Declan? It's too much for them and they each have some of the ancient gifts. You don't. It will consume you."

"You didn't give it to them because it's my place as the elder to help you. Give it to me!"

The two brothers stared at each other in silence. Layton could feel Brandon trying to marshal his pain. He could see the losing struggle in Brandon's eyes. He took a deep breath and then reached out and grasped Brandon's hand.

At the touch, a wall of despair surged along Brandon's arm and rushed into Layton, nearly overwhelming him. He felt Brandon's vain effort to hold it back.

Layton closed his eyes. He gasped, trying to absorb wave after wave of pure, unadulterated pain. Despite his efforts, he knew its relentless assault would soon engulf him.

He felt Brandon tugging at his hand. *It's too much for you, Hawk. Let go!*

He tightened his grip on Brandon's and gritted his teeth. *Never!*

Let go before it consumes you. I can contain it and draw it back if you let go now! Please, Hawk!

If I let go it will consume you!

If you don't, it will consume us both!

So be it! I'm not letting go!

Just as he thought both he and Brandon would be consumed, Layton felt two familiar presences and then a hand clamp on his shoulder. The wall of despair slowly devouring him and Brandon abated until it was a dull but bearable ache. He felt Brandon summoning it back. The remnant of despair flowed down Layton's arm and rushed back into Brandon.

Brandon's hand was pulled from his. Free of the tight constriction that had been squeezing his lungs, Layton fell backward, struggling to breathe. An arm slid around his shoulder, steadying him.

He opened his eyes and smiled up at his younger brother. "Declan."

Declan looked pale but he smiled. "Hawk."

Layton turned his head and saw Bancroft, looking as pale as Declan. He knelt on the floor. He had one arm around Brandon's shoulder. His right hand clasped Brandon's. Both brothers' eyes were closed and they both shook.

Layton rose, swayed and felt Declan behind him. "They'll be all right, Hawk. They just need to be alone for awhile." Declan put an arm around his shoulder. "You're weak. Let's get you to bed."

"I'm fine, Declan."

"No, you're not fine. You've absorbed far more negative energy than you should have. You're going to need some time to allow it to bleed off."

"What about you?"

Declan smiled. "I'm a little weak too but I'm used to this. You're not."

Layton glanced over at Brandon and Bancroft, who were now clinging to each other but still shaking. "What about them? What about Brandon? What about you? Both you and Bancroft are pale."

Declan turned him toward the door. "God willing, Croft will be okay. I'm fine. By the time we arrived, you had already absorbed most of Brandon's pain. We just ensured it didn't consume you both. Brandon's still hurting but thanks to you, at least now his pain is going to be manageable. Now he has a chance to be happy again."

"I don't know about that, Declan. He really loved her."

"I know he did but most of his pain was driven by guilt. You absorbed most of that. He now has a chance to be happy again—if he meets his *sheenea*."

"Risssa was—"

"I know but who says there can only be one?"

"There was only one for mother. And because of that her spirit will never know true peace."

"Brandon's not here and right now, I'm more concerned about you."

"Me?"

"Yes. You're carrying a large part of Brandon's guilt and pain now. That's a heavy burden, Hawk. You're going to need to learn how to handle it until it's dispersed by a more powerful, positive energetic force—like love. And I wouldn't be so sure mother's spirit is not at peace."

He stopped and stared at Declan. "She's at peace?"

Declan nodded.

"Are you sure?"

"I'm positive, Hawk. If I wasn't, I wouldn't say it."

Layton closed his eyes and released a long, shuddering breath.

Declan put a hand on his shoulder and he turned to embrace him.

"Now it's time to concentrate on Brandon and you. Once you regain your strength, you know what you need to do. Don't you?"

"Yes."

"And you'll do it?"

"Yes. I'll do it."

"It's going to be a while before all the darkness dissipates, Hawk."

"I know."

He hesitated. "And there's a chance that some of it may linger."

"For how long?"

"Forever. Sometimes it changes who we are forever, Hawk. You'll need to bear that in mind when you're with Tempest. Are you going to be okay with that?"

He nodded. "Yes. I had to try to help him. If this experience changes my relationship with Tempest, so be it. She's my *sheenea*. We'll get through any permanent changes together."

Declan nodded. "Yes. You will but for the moment, you're going to need to stay away from her."

He sighed. "I understand."

* * * * *

Layton made no effort to contact Tempest. By Friday night, Tempest's anger was beginning to give way to fear. Damn him for making her believe he cared for her and wanted her when all he'd wanted was unprotected sex—which she'd been all to willing to give him.

She spent the entire weekend at home. She feared the moment she left the apartment, Layton might call or visit. Each night she struggled to fall asleep, only to wake several times during the night longing for him.

She woke just before dawn on Monday morning. She was tired and dispirited and slowly coming to grips with the certainty that Layton couldn't possibly care about her. Yet she wanted him and was prepared to subjugate her pride to get him back in her bed.

She got out of bed, showered, had a light breakfast and dressed. The phone rang as she was on her way to work. The caller ID indicated it was one of the phones in Layton's mansion. Finally. She snatched up the receiver. "Hello?"

"Hi."

For a moment, her heart raced and she was in danger of hyperventilating. Then she realized that although the voice was familiar, it wasn't quite as warm or as deep as Layton's. "Brandon?'

"Yes."

She closed her eyes and leaned against the wall, fear racing through her. "Oh no," she whispered. "Where is he? What's wrong? Is he all right? Oh Brandon, please tell me he's all right."

There was an agonizing pause before he spoke. "If you mean Hawk, he's been better."

She bit her lip and sucked in a breath. "What's happened? Where is he?"

"He's in some distress. He needs to see you. Will you go to him?"

"Yes! Where is he? Oh Brandon, tell me what's happened."

"He's home but he's an emotional wreck."

She sucked in an angry breath. "Home? Did you say he's home?"

"Yes but he's an emotional wreck."

"Is he ill? Has he been in an accident?"

141

He sighed. "No but—"

"Then he'll be a physical wreck when I get my hands on him!"

He responded in a soft, soothing voice. "You're angry."

"What was your first damned clue?"

"If you need to talk—"

"What I need is to have your thoughtless, woman chasing, heart-breaking, no-good, cheating brother out of my life!"

"Please don't say that."

"What's his damned problem, Brandon? Why has he been avoiding me after he…" She paused and compressed her lips. "Why are you calling instead of him? Did he ask you to call?"

"No. He doesn't know I'm calling."

"Then why are you calling?"

"I know you're probably feeling…abandoned. Without betraying him, I wanted to try and explain what's going on with him."

"As much as I like you, Brandon, you're not the Grayhawk I'm interested in talking to at the moment."

"I understand that. I just want to do all I can to ensure he doesn't blow things with you just because he's not thinking straight. He needs you, Tempest. Will you go see him?"

"Why should I?"

"I was hoping you'd be a better man than him."

"Well I'm not!"

"You may not believe this but I know he cares about you and I suspect you care about him. Given that fact, does it really matter which one of you makes the first move?"

Why the hell did everyone keep asking her that? "How many times am I supposed to chase him?"

"Love doesn't keep track of who's right or who's wrong."

"Maybe not but if he wants anything more than what he's already had, he's going to have to make the first move this time!" She felt an ache in her heart at the thought that he wouldn't care enough to do that. "When you talk to him again, tell him that I'm through listening to his lies."

"Trust your heart, Tempest. Delve into your feelings honestly. When you do, you'll have to admit you know he didn't lie to you about his feelings and you'll know he hasn't been unfaithful to you."

"What I know, Brandon, is that I'm not chasing him again. If he wants me and our...if he wants me, he'll have to come to me this time."

"You know he wants you."

"Then where the hell has he been for the last seven days?"

"You're not the only one who is confused. More, he's afraid, honey. Can't I convince you to stretch out your hand to him?"

"Not before hell freezes over, Brandon!" She broke the connection and turned off the ringer.

Damn Layton. First he made her believe he was practically in love with her, made her crave his love and attention and then he avoided her. When she decided she wanted but didn't need him, he had Brandon try to intercede for him. He was afraid? She doubted he knew the meaning of the word. What he felt was regret that he'd led her to believe he felt more for her than he did. Now he was afraid to face her and expected her to subjugate what was left of her pride and go running after him again.

Layton's car was in his space when she arrived at work. Resisting the urge to slam her fist on the hood and dent the damned car he was so fond of, she went to her office. The day dragged. Every time her phone rang or someone knocked on her office door she was on tenterhooks. The workday ended without her encountering Layton.

The next four days passed in much the same fashion. On Friday afternoon, she said her goodbyes to her staff and left without having seen Layton.

Determined not to spend the evening alone thinking about him, she called Benai. "I need to talk."

"I was just about to toss a salad and bake a potato. I'll make enough for two and be over there in forty minutes."

"Thanks."

Over dinner, she and Benai talked about everything except Layton. Around ten Tempest started yawning.

Benai put her coffee cup down. "I'd better go and let you get to bed."

Tempest shook her head. "I'm all right."

"Actually, I don't think you're going to be all right until you make peace with Layton."

Tempest compressed her lips. "Why should I be the one to make the first move? He's not the one who's pregnant! I am!"

Benai's dark eyes widened. "Are you sure?"

"I took two home pregnancy tests this morning. Even before I did, though, I knew I was pregnant."

"You two are going to have a baby together. Why does it matter who makes the first move?"

"What?"

"You were the one who didn't want to talk about a permanent commitment when he broached the subject."

"But that was only because I wasn't sure of him!"

"You probably injured his pride. If I were you, I wouldn't let a little thing like pride stand between me and the man I love."

"Maybe I'm not in love with him."

"Don't hand me that line, girl. Even as an inexperienced virgin, you had enough sense to make Brian use protection."

"I wish I hadn't. If I hadn't, maybe we'd have had a child."

"You're going to have a child, Temp. Layton's child. So don't tell me you don't love him."

Tempest shook her head.

"Do you want me to talk to him?"

Benai's offer surprised her. "I didn't know you and he were that close, Nai."

"We're not. Our relationship is strictly professional. He's always polite and considerate when we meet. Even as he's asking how I am and how business is, I always know he's just being courteous. I was offering to talk to him on your behalf."

"Thanks, Nai but that wouldn't work with him."

"Is there anything I can do or say to help?"

"You've already done it."

Benai rose and bent to kiss Tempest's cheek. "Get a good night's sleep and in the morning, get your butt on the phone and tell him how you feel and let true love and nature take their course."

"If I thought he loved me, I would."

"If I thought he didn't, I wouldn't suggest it, Temp. If you really love him and you think he's a good man, let him win. Even handsome hunks like him sometimes have fragile egos. What would it hurt to let him win this round?"

"Nai—"

Benai grinned. "Just think how good he'll look in that black cowboy hat—provided it can fit that oversized head of his."

Tempest frowned. "Hey, girl! His head is not oversized!"

Benai laughed. "Isn't it? Then let him win so we can get on with enjoying your pregnancy." She squeezed Tempest's hand. "Think about it. Okay?"

She nodded. "I will."

After Benai left, Tempest took a hot soak before bed. Although she was tired, she lay awake for what felt like hours. Finally, mentally and physically exhausted, she fell into an uneasy slumber filled with nightmares of never seeing Layton again.

She woke drenched in sweat, shaking with fear and sure of what she wanted and needed. Despite his stubborn streak and determination to have his way, Layton was a good man. He'd be an excellent father to their child. She caressed her belly. She needed to do what was best for her baby as well as herself.

Tempest had toast, scrambled egg whites and orange juice for breakfast, before she showered and dressed. Before her courage could desert her, she left the apartment. As she opened the lobby door, she encountered Layton.

They stared at each other in silence for several moments. Then he smiled. "Hi, honey."

Her heart raced and she had to fight to keep a flood of tears at bay. "Layton!"

He put an arm around her shoulders and urged her back into the lobby. "We need to talk."

She nodded.

"Where were you going, Tempest?"

Should she admit she'd been on her way to see him? Or should she let him lay his feelings bare first?

"Tempest?"

She swallowed and spoke quickly. "I was on my way to see you."

He smiled. "Great minds think alike. As you can see, I've come to see you."

His attempt at humor annoyed her. "Where have you been, Layton?"

His smile vanished. "I haven't seen you in two weeks. Where do you think I've been?"

"I have no idea."

"I've been in hell."

She sucked in an angry breath. "Oh *you've* been in hell. Where do you think I've been?"

He caressed her cheek. "I'm sorry."

She shook her head and stepped away from him. "I don't want to hear you're sorry. I want to know where you've been."

"I told you. In hell."

She noted the bleak look in his dark eyes and swallowed the urge to ask him if he'd been alone. "Don't they have phones there?"

He laughed and wrapped his arms around her. "We need to talk."

"You're starting to repeat yourself." She drew away from him. "You have a lot of explaining to do."

"I know."

"Well, I'm waiting."

He slipped his arm around her shoulders again. "I came prepared to fall on my sword if that's what you want."

"What I want is to slap you until your face stings."

"I know." He walked her over to the locked door leading to the elevators. She used her keycard to open it and he walked her through. He pushed the elevator call button before he turned her to face him. "Let's go upstairs and talk."

She stared at him. She felt angry and hurt that he'd ignored her for so long but also happy and elated that he hadn't waited for her to make the first move. He had come to her—finally.

"Tempest? Honey?"

She slipped her arm around his waist and curled her fingers in his jacket. Then she turned her face against his shoulder. "I hate you!"

He dropped a quick kiss against her hair. "I hope not because if you really do I'm going to be screwed big time."

She lifted her head and looked up at him. "Why did you do this to me? I thought you cared about me."

He caressed her cheek. "I think you know I do...or you wouldn't have been on your way to see me."

"Are you going to gloat because you won?"

"Won? You were on your way to see me. I'm already here. If anyone won, I'd say it was you. Now, can we go upstairs to talk?"

She nodded.

Chapter Ten
ഔ

Once in her apartment, she sat on the loveseat watching him pace the living room floor. Finally, he stopped by the window and turned to look at her. "Why were you coming to see me?"

She shook her head. "Oh no! You're the one who've been avoiding me for nearly two weeks. You start."

He sighed. "You want your pound of flesh?"

She lifted her chin and glared at him. "Every damned ounce."

He stared at her silently, his lowered lids masking his expression.

She sighed. "Unless, of course, you don't care enough to—"

"Oh I care, all right. Damn you, Tempest! You know I care. I have almost from the moment we met."

"What? But that was—"

"I'm well aware of how long it's been since we met." He raked a hand through his hair. "It's been a very long time for me, Tempest."

Even with the expression in his eyes hidden from her, she heard the sincerity in his voice. "If you're so..." She paused and bit her lip. "Are you in love with me?"

He nodded. "Yes. I'm in love with you."

She closed her eyes and savored the words, replaying them in her mind. *Yes. I'm in love with you.*

She felt his fingers on her face and opened her eyes. He knelt in front of her. His lids were up. His feelings were clear for her to read in his expression. The tears that had pricked her eyes, spilled down her cheek. "You love me?"

"I don't just love you. I'm in love with you too."

"Oh Layton! Are you sure?"

"I've been sure for a very long time."

"How long?"

He shrugged. "I've loved you from the moment we met. It took a little longer to fall so deeply in love with you that I'll never be able to love anyone else." He wiped her tears away. "The moment I saw you, part of me knew you were my soul mate or as my mother would say, I knew you were my *sheenea*."

"Sheena?"

"Not Sheena. *Sheenea*."

"*Sheenea*?" The word had a lovely, romantic feel. "Is that Cherokee? "

"I think the word is far older than the Cherokee nation is. It binds one individual to another for life, hence the term life mate." He stroked her cheeks. "You are my *sheenea*, Tempest, the one woman in the world who completes me. I don't just love you. I need you. Without you I'm incomplete."

"Oh Layton! I think I'm in love with you like that too."

He swore and shook his head. "You *think*? You only *think*?"

She squeezed his hand. "No. I know."

He exploded to his feet and paced the floor. "It's about damn time!" He swung around to face her. "What took you so damned long, Tempest? Couldn't you feel how I felt about you every time we were together?"

"No! And even if I had suspected how you felt, there was nothing to do about it while you were married."

"Well, I'm not married now."

"No, you're not." She rose and opened her arms. "I need a hug."

He wrapped his arms around her and pressed his cheek against hers.

He shuddered against her.

She rubbed his back. "It's all right." Even as she whispered the words, she felt a hint of doubt. He seemed different—almost as if a dark cloud had descended on him. "Layton? What's wrong?"

His arms tightened around her. "Nothing."

"I can feel a difference in you, Layton."

He shuddered again. "I'll be all right but I need a hell of a lot more than a hug."

"I'm ready to give you whatever you need."

He drew away from her and gazed into her eyes. "Are you sure?"

"Yes, I'm sure but just tell what's wrong."

"Later." He swept her off her feet and into his arms.

She linked her arms around his neck and pressed her cheek against his shoulder as he carried her down the hall to her bedroom. He set her on her feet.

She caressed his cheeks. "Layton? Please tell me what's wrong?"

"I need you now." He rained kisses on her face as he unbuttoned her coat and tossed it onto the bed. He reached for her blouse.

She shook her head and sat on the side of the bed. "Can we have a quick talk first?"

He groaned, shook his head and started pulling off his clothes. "Later."

"No, Layton. Now. We need to talk now."

Standing in his briefs, he paused and stared at her. "What can't wait a little while longer, Tempest?"

"I want to know why you spent the entire last two weeks avoiding me when I have a feeling you knew how I felt."

"I guarantee you that if I'd known how you felt for certain, we would never have spent the last two weeks apart. I stayed away because I was afraid I was still in love alone. Brandon assured me that wasn't the case."

"And you didn't believe him?"

"I wanted to but I've never been in love before. I've been in lust but never in love. I was trying to figure out how I could get you to marry me if our baby is a boy."

She blinked. "Aren't you assuming a lot?"

"That you're pregnant?" He shook his head. "I know you're pregnant."

"How do you know?"

"Brandon told me."

"When?"

"Saturday before last."

"Saturday before…how could he possibly have told you then? I didn't even know for certain until I took a pregnancy test yesterday morning and it still has to be confirmed by a doctor."

He shrugged. "Sometimes he knows things. The only thing he didn't know was the sex of the baby."

"If you knew I was pregnant, why did you avoid me?"

He sighed. "I've already told you. I was afraid I was still in love alone. I thought that if I stayed away and you called me, I'd know I at least had a chance."

"What made you come today?"

"I love you and I couldn't stay away any longer. I decided we were so good together in bed because we were meant to be together. And I realized it was time I stopped trying to wait you out and started acting like you're my life mate and the woman I'd walk barefoot over hot coals for."

"Barefoot over hot coals, huh?"

He nodded.

"But can't you Native American hunks do that without breaking a sweat?"

He arched a brow. "Maybe Declan could pull that off without having the soles of his feet burned to a crisp. Brandon and Bancroft are so intuitive that they would know which coals were more bare-feet friendly resulting in as little damage as possible. Randall and Peyton are so driven, they could both probably *will* their feet not to burn or blister. But I don't possess any of the ancient abilities that many of my siblings do. So with me, we're talking burned to a well-done crisp."

"Then it would hurt you?"

"To put it mildly, yes."

"Would you really do that?"

He nodded, locking his gaze on hers. "Yes, I would."

"I think I believe you."

"Good because I mean it. And to prove it, I came prepared to admit how I feel and to beg you to marry me."

"Marry you?"

He picked up his jacket from the floor. He crossed the room to the bed and knelt at her feet. "Yes." He opened his palm, revealing a small, black jeweler's box.

She bit her lip. "What's in it?"

"Open it and see."

"Is it an engagement ring?"

"You know how to find out."

She opened it and saw a beautiful white gold diamond solitaire. "Oh Layton, it's gorgeous."

"So are you, my love."

"Oh Layton."

"Will you marry me?"

"Yes! Oh yes, Layton!" She nodded and thrust out her hand. "Of course I'll marry you."

He slipped the ring on her finger before he hugged her. "Thank God."

She clung to him, raking her hands down his back.

He held her in silence for several moments before he drew away from her. He wiped her cheeks. "Now can we make love?"

She could still sense a disturbing darkness in him but she decided to allow him to share the cause for it with her in his own time. "No wonder women have been chasing you for years. You have a silver tongue."

He grinned. "Would you like to feel what I can do with it?"

"Oh yes."

He practically ripped off his clothes, then sat on one of the leather chairs by the window, watching her undress more slowly.

She did a slow striptease for him.

As he watched her wiggling her ass and holding her breasts, he slowly pumped his cock.

When it stood at attention, she licked her lips. "See anything you like, handsome?"

"Oh yes. Damn, honey, you are so beautiful."

She smiled. "Yeah?"

He parted his legs. "Hell, yeah."

"Which part of me do you like best?"

"I like everything about you starting with that beautiful chocolate skin of yours...your large, luscious breasts...your long, shapely legs...your gorgeous round ass...but your crowning jewel is your shaved pussy."

She walked across the room to straddle him.

"Sit on me," he whispered in a brusque voice.

She stroked her fingers through his hair. "Didn't I hear something about your showing me what you could do with that silver tongue of yours?"

"Later. Right now I just need to feel you all around me."

She sank onto his lap.

He leaned forward and kissed her forehead, her eyelids and her cheeks. "I need you."

Her lips parted in a silent sigh as tiny embers of pleasure danced through her at the feel of his tender caresses.

He kissed her breasts. "I love you."

Her heart swelled and her eyes welled with tears. "Oh Layton, I love you too."

He licked her face, slowly moving the tip of his tongue along her cheek to her right ear. He whispered something soft and haunting. Cherokee. Although she didn't understand the other words, she heard the word *sheenea*. That sent a nice warm shiver through her. Although she didn't understand the other words, she liked the fact that he felt the need to speak his native tongue while making love to her. It served to strengthen the bond forming between them.

She slipped her fingers in his hair and turned her head until their mouths touched. A jolt of pleasure sizzled through her. She eagerly licked his lips. "Kiss me."

He circled her parted lips with the tip of his tongue. As he did, he rotated his hips against hers, grinding his cock against her slit. He hardened against her. It wouldn't be long before she felt him sliding into her. Soon he would be filling her with the delicious fullness she had only experienced when they made love. She moaned, her love tempered by an insatiable hunger for sex with him.

He reached between their bodies and stroked her slit. "There's my pretty baby."

She kissed his mouth. "My pussy is happiest when it's mated with your dick."

"Show me."

She rose and reached down to cup his cock. Pointing it toward her slit, she eased her hips downward.

His shaft parted her slit and slipped inside. He gripped her hips. "Oh yeah, baby."

"Yeah, baby," she repeated. She licked her lips and pinched her nipples as she felt the exquisite penetration of his cock. "Oh Layton, you feel so good sliding in so slow and so deep."

His hands tightened on her waist. "Take it all, baby…every inch."

"Yes. Oh yes." She sank down onto his lap with his cock buried inside her.

He groaned, palmed her ass and buried his face between her breasts. "My cock and your pussy are a match made in heaven."

She cupped his cheeks and urged his head up from her breasts so she could gaze into his eyes. "Yes, my love, heaven."

"Ride me, baby."

She linked her arms around his neck and rode him hard, grinding her pussy around the base of his cock.

He sighed softly and bent his head to her breasts.

She slipped a hand behind his head to keep his warm lips moving against her tight nipples.

That felt so good but she wanted more. She settled into a steady rhythm that sent pleasant little jolts through her each time she slammed her ass onto his hard thighs. He pushed his hips upward, forcing his cock up into her.

Oh yes!

When he abruptly lifted his right hand and slapped her ass, she experienced a flash of pleasure so intense that she gasped and arched into him. He lifted his head from her breast. "You like having your beautiful, brown ass slapped?"

"No. Oh no. I don't like it at all."

He laughed and slapped her other cheek hard. "Still don't like it? What about now? And now?"

"Oh...I...hate it!" She whimpered and squirmed in delight as he rained delicious, sharp slaps to her stinging, quivering ass cheeks.

Shocked that she liked having her ass spanked, she shuddered, crushed her breasts against his chest and sought his mouth.

As they kissed and fucked, he continued to rain hard smacks down on her ass. Each whack on her now tender flesh sent her soaring closer to an explosive orgasm. Her release came in the midst of a series of relentless blows to her butt. She sobbed out his name and came all over his big, hard cock.

Gripping her hips, he sucked the side of her neck and thrust into her for several more minutes before he exploded inside her. Then he collapsed back against the chair, holding her close.

Sighing softly, she pressed her cheek against his damp shoulder. "Layton?"

"Yes?"

"Is this real? Am I dreaming or are you really mine?"

He squeezed her. "I'm yours forever, *sheenea*." He whispered something softly in Cherokee. She didn't understand the words, but she liked the sound of them and the affection in his voice.

Feeling sexually sated and wonderfully cherished and loved, she fell asleep with him still inside her.

Later, he carried her to bed where she stumbled back into his arms and drifted to sleep again.

She woke late in the afternoon to the smell of meat and vegetables cooking. Her stomach rumbled. She slipped out of bed, pulled on a robe and went into the kitchen.

Layton stood at the stove, dressed only in his trousers.

She stood in the doorway of the kitchen admiring the lines of his shoulders and back before stepping into the room. "Hmmm. Something smells scrumptious."

He turned and smiled at her. "Damn, you look even more beautiful after you've been making love."

She smiled and walked across the room. She wrapped her arms around his waist and kissed his shoulder. "It's because I'm in love."

He lifted her chin. "Yeah? With anyone I know?"

She shook her head. "Nope."

He slapped her ass.

"Ouch!" She wiggled out of his arms and stepped around him to look into the saucepans. One contained corn, green beans and carrots simmering in a dark broth. Another contained baked chicken. Still another contained brown rice.

She grinned at him. "He's sexy, handsome, a fantastic lover and he cooks? How is it that some lucky woman hasn't married you?"

He pulled a chair out from the table. "I was saving myself for you."

She sank into it. "Lucky me."

He returned to the stove. Moments later, he placed two plates on the table, one in front of her and the other across from her.

"What would you like to drink?"

"Orange juice with ice."

He moved toward the refrigerator. "Bread or rolls?"

"Rolls but I can get it."

"No. You stay seated." When he returned to the table, he kissed the back of her neck. "You'll need to save your strength for love making."

She smiled and picked up her fork. "This doesn't seem real."

He grimaced. "Don't you start that shit again, Tempest. This is as real as it gets."

She placed her fork beside her plate, broke off a corner of a roll and nibbled at it. "I just meant…I know why I'm in love with you but why are you in love with me?"

"Why wouldn't I love you?"

"You can have any woman you want."

"I want and need you. I knew the moment I saw you I'd made a big mistake with Allison."

"Then why did you stay married to her for years after we met?"

"I knew it in my heart but it took me a while to admit it. By the time I had, you were seeing someone. I thought it was serious so I thought I might as well stay married to Allison."

"Why?"

"If I couldn't have you, what difference did it make who I shared my bed with?"

"But what was it about me that made you fall in love with me?"

"Aside from beauty?"

She sat back in her chair, a wide smile spreading across her face. He clearly really believed she was beautiful. "Yes. Aside from that."

He shrugged. "My mother used to always say that for most people, there's only one true love and we'd know it when it came along. After watching her lose her spark and joy in life when my father started cheating, I didn't believe it. The moment we met, I knew she was right."

"How?"

"I don't know. I just know there was something cold and implacable inside me that no other woman had been able to touch. That nameless something burst into a roaring flame the moment I saw you. But I'm not at my brightest when I'm in love, so it took me a while to admit that you were the one and only love of my life."

Her eyes swelled with tears. "Oh Layton! You are the sweetest man I've ever known."

"Really? What about your Brian?"

She shook her head. "He was the love of my life and my reason for living." She watched myriad emotions flash across Layton's face, anger, jealousy and fear. "Layton, I—"

"Your reason for living? Where does that leave me, Tempest?"

She rose, walked around the table and linked her arms around his neck. "I loved him with all the angst of young, untried love and he will always have a warm place in my memories." She brushed her lips against his cheek. "But he is a part of my past. You are my future, Layton." She sank onto his lap and looked into his eyes. "You and our baby will be my new reason for living."

She kissed his lips. "I won't forget him but he is my past. The love I felt for him was real and strong but it was the love of a girl." She caressed his cheek. "I'm a woman now and I offer you the love of a woman. Please don't feel you have to be jealous of his memory."

He sighed and pressed his forehead against hers. "How can I be sure you're not just settling for me because he's gone?"

She cupped his face and lifted his head. "I can promise that you have my heart and soul and that you have them forever. My love for you is more mature and deeper than what I felt for him. I'll do my best to ensure your nights of desire are over forever."

He stared at her.

"I love you, Layton and I'll spend the rest of forever making sure you know that. Is that enough?"

"When did you know you loved me?"

"I think, on a subconscious level, I've known it for a few years but I couldn't admit it to myself. Recently when I woke from a restless sleep and realized that I no longer had any desire or interest in naming our baby after Brian, I knew I'd finally moved on from what I felt for him because I loved you with my entire being. So? Is it enough?"

He buried his face against her breasts. "Yes. It's enough."

But she sensed a trace of uncertainty in him. She stroked his hair. "So. Do you think we'll be calling our first baby Layton or Laytonia?"

He jerked his head up and stared at her. "Lay...what happened to Brian or Brianna?"

She studied his face. "Would that work for you?"

He briefly averted his gaze, sighed and then looked into her eyes. "If that's what you want...yes."

"It's not what I want." She smiled and caressed his face. "There's no reason for our first child to be named after anyone but his father. Brian was a sweet man and he would have wanted me to move on and be happy with the man of my choice. And that's you, Layton."

His dark gaze searched hers. "Are you sure? Because if you really want to name the baby Bri—"

She pressed her fingers against his lips. "I'm very sure."

He hugged her and buried his face against her neck. He whispered softly to her in Cherokee.

"You're going to have to teach me Cherokee."

He lifted his head to look at her. "Gladly, darling."

"Now, wait I have a present for you."

He lifted his head, his eyes gleaming. "Yeah?"

She laughed. "Not that. I mean a real present."

He grinned. "That is a real present."

"Be serious." She rose. "Stay there and I'll be back with your present." She went back to her bedroom. She lifted a hatbox from the top shelf of her walk-in closet and returned to the kitchen.

He arched a brow and patted his lap.

She straddled him, holding the hatbox near her side. "This is for you."

He took the box and removed the top.

She watched his lips curve in a smile as he lifted the big, black hat from the box. He examined it in silence.

She took it from him and put it on his head. "Wow. I knew you would look great in this. Will you wear it?"

"I'm not really a hat guy, honey."

She linked her arms around his neck. "But you look so sexy in it. And when you wear it with jeans and the black boots I bought—"

"Black boots! You bought black boots?"

She nodded. "I was only going to get the hat but I kind of got carried away. Promise you'll wear them."

He groaned.

She pushed the hat onto the back of his head. "Promise."

"I promise I'll wear the hat—occasionally...maybe."

"And the boots?"

"Don't press your luck," he warned.

"Okay. I'll settle for your wearing the hat occasionally and we'll work on the boots later."

"God save me from a pushy woman who wants to dress me like a hillbilly."

She laughed but sobered quickly. "Tell me what's bothering you now?"

He sighed. "I don't want to scare you."

"I want to know what's going on with you because whatever affects you affects me and our baby."

"Okay. It's Brandon."

Noting the bleak look in his eyes, she offered him her hand. He engulfed her hand in his.

She listened as he spoke in a soft, almost inaudible voice, frequently squeezing her hand.

He paused after several minutes, sighed and gave her a brief smile. "So you see why I didn't come before today?"

She nodded. "How is Brandon and the others?"

"Brandon is healing and the others are... There might be an issue with Bancroft, but we'll deal with that later." He sighed.

"Am I forgiven?"

"Of course you are. I wish I'd known. I could have sat with you. Why didn't you call me?"

"I didn't want to burden you."

"Burden me? It wouldn't have been a burden. I want to share everything with you. Don't shut me out again."

"I won't."

"What about Brandon? Is he all right?"

"Bancroft and Declan say it will take time for the healing process to begin but that he'll be all right eventually."

"Good. Are you sure you're all right? I can feel the difference in you."

He nodded. "I know. I feel like I'm carrying a dark center around. Declan assures me it will dissipate over time. Can you handle the new me until then?"

"Let me put it this way, handsome, even if you came with a heart as black as coal, I'd still want you."

He engulfed her in a bear hug, pressing his face against her neck.

She nibbled on his ear. "Hey. Can I interest you in a healing fuck?"

"Yes." He set her on her feet and rose.

Chapter Eleven
⬥

The phone rang.

He groaned. "Someone has lousy timing."

She laughed and picked up the receiver. "Hello?"

"Hi."

She smiled at the sound of the warm, male voice on the other end. "Hi."

"You sound good, honey. Is everything okay?"

"Things have never been better."

"So Hawk's there?"

"Yes, he is."

"Oh great."

Her other line beeped. "Hold on a second." She clicked on the other line. "Hello?"

"Temp, I just wanted to check to see if you're okay."

"Nai! I'm fine. Layton's here and everything is wonderful."

"Oh Temp, I knew he'd come through. I'll let you go."

"Before you do, I should tell you that Brandon's on the other line."

"And?"

"Oh Nai, don't you think it's like a sign? Both of you calling at almost the same time to make sure I'm all right?"

"A sign?"

"Yes. That the two of you should at least meet."

"Maybe. We'll talk later."

"Okay. Bye." She brought Brandon back on the line. "Brandon? Do you need to talk to Layton?"

"No. I just wanted to make sure he was there."

"And if he hadn't been?"

"I'd have had to go get him and drag his big, dumb ass there."

She frowned. "Hey! I happen to like his ass."

"Yeah, well, there's no accounting for taste. You take care, Tempest."

"I will. You do the same."

"I will."

"If you need to talk, Brandon, I'll be available to listen."

"Thanks, honey. I'll bear that in mind. Talk to you soon."

"Bye." She put the phone down and turned to face Layton. "That was Brandon. He wanted to make sure you were here."

"Nosey ass."

"You don't mean that."

"No. I don't. Brandon is… I love all my siblings very much but Brandon and I are…he's not just my brother, he's my best friend."

She walked over to him and wrapped her arms around his waist. "Then it's fitting he be the first to know about our baby."

He nodded. "Yes but right now I have something else in mind besides talking about his big, dumb ass."

She smiled up at him, stroking her hands over his chest. "And what might that be?"

He swept her off her feet. "Let me show you."

"Yes," she whispered. "Please do."

Several minutes later, she lay on her back in bed with Layton on top of her. As he took her slowly, he sucked her breasts.

165

With her pussy flooding, she thrust her hips up against his. "Layton...oh, Layton, I love you."

He silenced her with a warm, demanding kiss full of tenderness and passion. While she drowned in the sweet heat of his desire, he rolled them onto their sides. He withdrew his cock. Her instinctive protest at the lost of his weight and his dick died on her lips as she felt his fingers parting her outer folds. Deepening his kiss, he probed her wet slit before he circled and then rubbed his thumb against her clit.

A shock of pleasure sizzled through her. She gasped, feeling an almost unbearable sexual tension and need for release building in the pit of her stomach. She moistened her lips and then parted them in a shameless display of hunger.

Taking advantage of her open mouth, he French kissed her.

She pushed her tongue into his mouth and shuddered when he sucked it.

One long finger slipped inside her pussy...thrusting...probing...nice...so nice. She wiggled her hips and moaned softly as a second digit found its way inside her. He slid his fingers in and out of her while he devoured her mouth...branding the taste and feel of his lips and tongue on hers.

Sweet, delicious pleasure buffeted her senses. Curling her fingers in his hair, she wildly humped herself on his fingers, her stomach muscles rippling and tightening. When he tore his mouth away from hers, he licked and kissed a slow, burning path down to her breasts.

As he did, he nibbled on her skin and whispered to her in Cherokee. Every now and then she clearly heard the word *sheenea*. Her nipples pebbled and the embers in her belly flared. At the touch of his lips and tongue against her breasts, the embers warming in her belly sparked and flamed. Still thrusting into her, he rubbed her clit hard.

"Layton...oh, Layton!" She clutched his shoulders, wildly humping on his fingers as a powerful climax rushed over her. While she was still caught up in the rapture of her release, he rolled her onto her back, parted her legs and tilted her hips upward. Kneeling between her thighs, he pressed his open mouth over her climaxing pussy. The feel of his tongue and teeth nibbling and licking at her heightened and prolonged her pleasure.

She shoved his face tight against her slit and savored the delight of him lapping up her release as she came. He kept his lips and tongue in motion until the last shudder of joy left her body.

Nice. So damned, fucking nice. But she wanted more.

She cupped her hands over her breasts, eager for more pleasure. "I want your cock again."

He rose. Pressing his body against her side, he caressed her face. "How badly do you want it?"

"So badly I ache with the need. Love me."

"Oh yes, baby."

She felt his cock, still hard and heavy against her thigh. Her stomach muscles tightened in anticipation. She opened her eyes and turned to face him. His dark eyes blazed with desire.

She caught her breath. No man had ever looked at her with such need before. The look made her feel as if she were the sexiest woman he'd ever been with. It empowered her, freeing her of any remaining inhibitions. Reaching between their bodies, she wrapped her fingers around his cock. She could feel pre-cum seeping from the big head.

She licked her lips, brushed her breasts against his chest and smiled with satisfaction when he inhaled sharply. She gently pumped him. "I need to feel this inside me."

He breathed deeply and began rotating his hips.

She leaned closer and teasingly circled the tip of her tongue along his mouth before she drew back and met his gaze

167

again. "I suppose now you want to stick this big, bad boy deep into my pussy, huh?"

He inched closer, pressing his big, heavy balls against her. "What makes you think that?" He demanded in a brusque whisper.

Staring into his eyes, she adjusted her grip on him and rubbed the warm helmeted head along her slit.

He tensed.

She smiled. "Just a lucky guess." She drew his dick head along her slit again, this time pressing the head briefly between her nether lips.

He sighed deeply, his hands closing over her waist.

"Doesn't this feel good?" She slid his cock along her lips again, this time dipping several inches of it briefly into her wet pussy.

He swore softly, his big hands tightening on her waist.

Pushing her legs further apart, she pressed his cock head against her clit several times, closing her eyes and moaning softly at the resultant sensations. "Oh that feels good."

He groaned. "No more."

She opened her eyes and blinked at him. "No more? But I—"

"It's not enough, Tempest!" His nostrils flared and he rolled her onto her back, pressed her legs apart with one knee and slid between her thighs.

She looked down. His hard shaft rested against her. Keeping his weight on his extended arms, he stared down at her, his lips parted, his tongue extended.

She slipped her hands along his shoulders. "What do you want?"

"Did I please you?"

She nodded, caressing his shoulders. "You know you did. You always do."

"Then it's my turn. I want your pussy and I want it hard and fast. Can you handle that?"

"I'm wet, still aroused and ready to give you whatever you want or need."

He took a deep breath. "I want to fuck you...consume you...make you mine forever."

She shivered in anticipation of the coming fuck. "Then do it."

He gripped his cock and thrust his hips downward.

She felt his big, hard, warm shaft penetrating her vagina. They had done this the night before. Yet it felt like the first time. She closed her eyes to relish the wonderful sensation of having him lodged just inside her.

He held still for several moments while she took long, deep breaths. Then, without warning, he drove his hips downward again. Several inches of hot, hard cock shot into her.

"Ooh!" She bit her lip and draped her legs over the back of his thighs. She took a moment to catch her breath before tilting her hips upward.

"That's my woman," he whispered and continued thrusting, driving the last few inches of his cock deep into her already-stretched tunnel.

"Oh yeah!" She wiggled her hips, wanting to feel every inch...every bit of him inside her. "Yes! Fuck me, Layton."

Sliding his hands under her to cup his palms over her ass, he withdrew half of his shaft. He pushed slowly back into her. Withdrawing again, he thrust back in harder and faster, only to withdraw again—this time leaving only the head inside her.

She moaned a protest and tightened her legs around him, jerking her hips upward. He pushed down, sending his shaft balls deep in her slick pussy. He started to fuck her then. Hard. Fast. Deep. So deep. So...delicious. He shot his length in and out of her with a passionate desperation that sent shivers of pleasure-pain sliding up and down her spine.

Good. Sooo good.

He fastened his lips on her right breast, swirled his tongue around her nipple and sucked hard.

Her pussy gushed and she arched into him, her world dissolving until he was at its center. Him. And his cock…thrusting and hurting…bringing pleasure and pain… Her entire world revolved around him and the almost unbearably delicious sensations he inflicted on her body and senses.

Even as he fucked her harder and harder, she lost herself in him. Physically he fucked her. On another, more important, spiritual level, he made love to her body and her mind. He touched deep-seated and hidden emotions that no man, not even Brian, had conquered. As she experienced a powerful orgasm, she felt the tiny detonations in her pussy as he came, jetting load after load of cum in her.

Moaning his name, she clung to him, raking her nails down his back until he collapsed on top of her, driving her hips back on the bed.

He whispered something soft against her ear, still inside her. *Sheenea.*

Feeling squashed by his weight, she held him, brushing her lips against his shoulder.

He nuzzled her ear. "Are you all right? Did I hurt you?"

"Yes," she admitted.

He sighed. "I'm sorry. I didn't mean to hurt you."

"Don't apologize, Layton. That was the most incredible experience of my life and I loved every second of it."

He turned his head and pressed a soft kiss against her lips. "I think I'm going to spend the rest of my life falling ever deeper in love with you every second of every day."

"Hmm. Is that line from another of your hillbilly songs?"

"Oh honey, one of these days you're going to have to learn to appreciate good music." He kissed her. "It's from my heart."

"No wonder if makes me feel so warm and fuzzy."

With his arms around her, he rolled them onto their sides, relieving her of his weight. He slipped behind her, cupped his hands over her breasts and cuddled close to her.

With the euphoria of their love making fading, reality returned. She knew a moment of fear. Although she was tired, she'd sleep better once she had been reassured about one last issue.

"Layton?"

"Yes?"

"We need to talk."

"Oh honey, can't it wait until later? Right now —"

"I need to talk now, Layton."

He sighed. "Okay. What's wrong?"

"If you knew I was the one for you the moment we met, why were all the women you dated after your divorce blondes? I can't remember a single one who looked anything like me."

He muzzled her neck before moving his lips against her ear. "I wanted you, Tempest, not someone who had the same skin color as you or the same hair texture. I deliberately didn't date anyone who looked anything like you because that would have only made not having you worse. The women I dated after my divorce were strictly to meet our joint sexual needs.

"I know it's not chivalrous to admit but none of them meant anything to me."

"There were so many of them, Layton."

He stroked her slit. "In case you haven't yet noticed, I have a strong sex drive. I like making love frequently. I wanted sex but I didn't want any relationship that would last long enough for my sexual partner to develop an emotional attachment I couldn't return. I didn't want to hurt anyone while waiting for you. That's why there were so many of them. I only dated them briefly to ensure there was no emotional attachment involved on either side. Does that make sense?"

She suspected one or more of his lovers had probably fallen for him but she was satisfied that he hadn't loved any of them. He'd probably broken more than his share of hearts but she doubted he had intentionally hurt anyone. Also, she believed he loved her with a depth of emotion she'd never expected. "I understand."

"Are you sure? I want you to be absolutely certain that you are the love of my life and I wouldn't change a single thing about you. You're perfect just as you are and I love you so much."

Any remaining doubts vanished. She loved Layton and he loved her. This was reality. With him at her side and in her bed, there would no longer be any need to escape into a world of fantasy. Lucky woman that she was, she was now going to get to live her fantasy with her lover and the father of her kids. Life didn't get any better.

Epilogue
ဢ

"Are you two decent? Can we come in?"

Tempest smiled. Layton, standing behind her, nibbling her ear, groaned. He lifted his head at the brisk knocking on the bedroom door, which followed the question.

"No, we're not decent and no you can't come in," Layton snapped in an annoyed voice. He shifted his hands from Tempest's waist to cup her breasts. "Go away."

Still wearing the dress Layton had paid a small fortune to have custom made in six weeks, she eased out of his arms. It had not been easy finding a wedding dress that would compliment a pregnant woman. Although she was only two months pregnant, the dress nicely concealed the slight swell to her belly. The seamstress had been worth every penny Layton had paid her. She'd hand-sewn a delicate English netting over the back and covered the short lace sleeves with embroidery. She had cleverly concealed the zipper behind a row of pearl buttons Benai had assured her had given her ample rear end a slenderizing appearance.

She smiled recalling the look of wonder on Layton's face when he'd turned in Randall's garden and seen her walking toward him in the beautiful ivory colored A-line style gown with its matching lace wrap and flowing train. She didn't want to risk Layton damaging it.

She turned to face him. Although he had removed the jacket of the black tuxedo, tossed his bowtie aside and unbuttoned several buttons of his skirt, he was otherwise dressed.

Layton tightened his arms around her and licked her lips. "Let's have a quickie."

Her heart raced. She was tempted but she knew that if she allowed Layton to undress her, they would be starting their honeymoon at Randall's mansion instead of in the Canary Islands. Besides, it felt almost decadent to even think about a quick fuck with a hundred plus guests dancing just a floor below.

She kissed Layton's lips. "I don't want our first time as a married couple to be a quickie, love."

He groaned, turning her in his arms so that he could kiss her nape.

"Tempest? It's Lelia."

Tempest resisted the temptation to rub her ass against his cock. She cleared her throat. "Yes, we're decent and yes you can come in, Lelia," she called. Ignoring Layton's fierce frown, she stepped around him as the bedroom door opened. Lelia Grayhawk, tall, with her long, almost black hair spilling over her slender shoulders and a happy smile on her beautiful face walked into the room, followed by Benai.

Lelia pressed a quick kiss against Layton's cheek. "Can we steal Tempest for a few moments?"

Tempest watched Layton give both women a long, cool look before he silently left the room.

Benai grimaced. "Ouch!"

Lelia stared after him for a moment before she looked at Benia. "I hope you don't misunderstand him. He didn't mean to be rude."

Benai smiled. "It's okay, Lelia. I know he has issues he's slowly working his way through."

"Good." She turned to smile at Tempest. "I have something special I wanted to give you before you left." She opened her handbag and removed a small, beautifully wrapped box about two inches wide and high.

Tempest took the box and removed the lid. Inside was a small, round jar, which seemed to contain a fragrant gel. She smiled at Lelia. "Thank you, Lelia. It has a wonderful fragrance. What is it?"

"The recipe has been passed down through the women in our family for generations. It's made from a combination of special herbs, spices and roots. We call it lover's balm. I don't know if it has any special properties but it's a tradition in our family to pass it on the wedding night to strengthen the long line of love."

Tempest stiffened. "The wedding night?"

Lelia's lips curved in a smile. "I know what you're thinking."

"You do?"

"Yes. You're thinking using it didn't help our mother."

Tempest felt her cheeks burn. "I wasn't thinking that." As she spoke, she lowered her lids.

"Of course you were but let me reassure you. She didn't use it on her wedding night."

"Why not?"

"There was no one to make it for her." Lelia sighed. "I'm not saying it would have made a difference but in our oral family history line on our mother's side, no one's ever been divorced."

Of course that raised yet another question.

Lelia, studying her face, shook her head slowly. "I didn't make it for Allison."

What a relief. "Why not?"

"Because I knew — we all knew she wasn't Hawk's *sheenea*. I wasn't about to waste my time and energies on a marriage everyone but Hawk knew wouldn't last. Any more questions?"

Tempest shook her head.

"Good. Now you just put a dash on either side of your neck, inside your wrists, your inner thighs and anywhere else you like some time today or tonight and watch Hawk go wild."

If Layton went any wilder than he'd been during the six weeks of their short engagement, he'd wear her out. "When should I apply it?"

"As with a perfume, the fragrance lasts for hours. You can either apply it now or later. It doesn't matter."

"Hmm. Then I might want to know where I can get more. Is it available from naturopathy stores?"

Lelia shook her head. "No. I made it myself from my mother's recipe. It takes weeks to make it just right."

"What about it will drive Layton wild?"

Lelia arched a brow. "Just knowing you cared enough to honor one of our many family traditions. It's a tradition the women in my mother's family have observed for generations...maybe longer."

"Longer than generations?"

Lelia nodded. "Our mother believed that our family has a very long history."

"How long?"

"Far longer than anyone alive can imagine."

"That long, huh?"

Lelia laughed. "Okay. I know what you're thinking here comes some mystic nonsense."

"You're quite the mind reader, aren't you?" She smiled. "No, I wasn't thinking that. I know some of you have abilities most of us would consider supernatural. Who's to say those abilities don't span the ages?"

Lelia smiled. "You are as wise as you are beautiful. No wonder Hawk fell in love with you. I knew the moment I saw you, I'd be making lover's balm."

Tempest blinked back a sudden rush of tears. "Knowing you cared enough to make this for me will make tonight even sweeter." She hugged Lelia. "Thank you."

Lelia kissed her cheek. "There's no thanks necessary. You're a Grayhawk now. That makes you the sister I've always longed for but never had. Welcome...sister."

The tears spilled down Tempest's cheeks. "Sister," she whispered.

"And since you are my only sister, I'll teach you to make it."

"That's touching, but why? I don't plan on ever loving or marring anyone else."

Lelia nodded. "I know, but I'm the only female in the family. When I meet my *sheenea*, I'll need you to make it for me to ensure my wedding night is as happy as I know yours and Hawk's will be."

"I'd love to do that for you."

Lelia squeezed her hand and left the room, closing the door behind her.

Tempest sank down onto the side of the bed, wiping her cheeks.

Benai sat beside her. "Wow, Temp. You look absolutely stunning."

She smiled. "So do you, Nai."

Benai grinned. "So. Has today been everything you hoped?"

She nodded. "Oh yes. Nai, I am so happy."

"You deserve to be."

"So do you." She tilted her head. "Did anything happen that I should know about while Layton and I have been in here?"

Benai grimaced. "If you mean has Brandon shown any interest in me, then no."

"I saw you two dancing."

"He was Layton's best man. I was your maid of honor. So he kind of had to dance with me at least once."

"He danced with you at least twice."

"Stop grasping at straws, Temp. He wasn't interested. In fact, to be honest, I found those two dances with him kind of invasive."

"In what way? Was he too intimate?"

"Far from it. There was nothing even remotely sexual in his touch. I know this will probably sound a little nuts but I got the feeling he was probing my thoughts."

"Oh. That." Tempest nodded. "Layton says that some of his siblings have what he calls ancient abilities. Apparently Brandon's touch can be somewhat probing or invasive."

"Well, I didn't like having him trying to get inside my head."

Tempest bit back a sigh. "I'll bet. How about Bancroft?"

Benai shrugged. "It's hard to believe he's the same guy who flirted with me so outrageously two months earlier."

Tempest sighed. "I told you about how Layton, Brandon and Bancroft are all a little different now."

"Different? Oh Temp, that's being really kind. If Bancroft got any cooler, I'd need gloves just to shake his hand. He's barely spoken to me all night. During both dances with Brandon, each time I looked up, I found Bancroft glaring at us." She sighed. "I have to admit that I kind of thought he was a little jealous but he soon set me straight on that score. When the dance was over, he walked past me and gave me a look so cold, I nearly shivered."

Tempest bit her lip. "He'll get better."

"Better? Temp, I think you need to face facts. Neither of those two is interested in me. He removed any remaining doubt when he finally asked me to dance."

"And?"

"And several times during the song, he just stopped and stood staring down at me, with the coldest look I've ever seen in a man's eyes. Each time I turned to walk away, he drew me back into his arms. I didn't know what to do without making a scene. The last time he did it, Randall came and asked if he could cut in. Bancroft practically tossed me at Randall and stalked off as if he couldn't get away from me fast enough."

Tempest heard the barely concealed confusion in Benai's voice and bit her lip. "I know things are difficult now, Nai. Things are hard for him too. Could you give him a little time?"

"Why would I?"

She hated it when Benai asked probing questions to which she didn't have an easy answer. "Well, when Layton first showed up at my door six weeks ago, the darkness in him was so pervasive, I could feel it. He's still not quite himself but he's much better now and he's getting better all the time. Bancroft will too."

Benai shrugged. "Maybe so but you're forgetting one very important difference. You have a vested interest in bearing with Layton. Even if either Bancroft or Brandon were interested in me, I have no motivation to try to wade upstream against the coldness they both project."

She squeezed Benai's hand. "Nai, they're both good men. I know either one of them would be worth the effort."

"I can't say that I agree with you, Temp." She brightened. "Oh a lighter note, that long dance with Randall helped get the circulation going again. Then, while I was trying to recover from dancing with such a hunk, I danced twice with Peyton."

"Twice? Then I guess you enjoyed the experience?"

"Enjoyed isn't the word. Have you danced with those two?"

Tempest grimaced. "Have I? I never thought dancing with hunks could be so exhausting."

"Have you felt the muscles they're packing?"

Tempest frowned. "I can't say I noticed. After I danced with Brandon and Bancroft, I just wanted to get through the other four dances as soon as possible." She hesitated. "So you danced twice with Peyton?"

Benai narrowed her gaze. "There's nothing happening there, Temp. Both he and Randall were being polite. I danced with him twice too."

"Randall doesn't strike me as the type to go out of his way to be polite."

Benai shrugged. "Really? I thought he was very nice."

"Just nice, huh?"

"Yes, Temp, just nice." She paused. "Nothing else."

She bit her lip. Was there a hint of excitement in Benai's voice? Did Benai want Randall to be more than polite? Or was Tempest just allowing her desire to see her best friend happy fill her head with fresh fantasies? She wasn't sure.

"Oh. Well, Layton says Randall and Payton are very driven. They're all successful in their chosen fields but Randall is the most financially successful and they're all very proud of him."

"I'm sure they have reason to be. Where'd he and Peyton get those gorgeous blue-green eyes?"

"It's strange, isn't it? He and Peyton have the same general bone structure and features as the other brothers but their eyes are different. Sometimes they look green, sometimes they look blue."

"Why?"

Tempest smiled. "Layton says they're not of this world."

"I'd sooner believe that of Brandon and Bancroft than Randall and Peyton."

Tempest studied her nails. "You know he's between women at the moment."

"Which one? Peyton..." Benai glanced down at her nails before looking up again. "Or Randall?"

Had Benai's voice softened when she mentioned Randall's name? "Both of them. They'd both be a great catch."

"Not for me."

Tempest stifled a sigh. So she wasn't interested in Randall after all. Or was she?

Benai slipped her arm through hers. "Don't worry about me. Even though nothing came of it, just having Bancroft flirt with me, was very good for the ego. I'll admit I was initially disappointed that he didn't follow through on all that flirting but trust me, I'm no longer interested in him. Now, I'm going to leave before Layton comes in here and drags me out so he can have you to himself." She kissed Tempest's cheek and rose.

Moments after she'd left, Bancroft appeared in the doorway. "Do you have a moment?"

Tempest nodded and patted the bed beside her.

He entered and closed the door.

For several moments, he sat silently beside her before he turned and looked at her.

Beneath the bleak look, she saw a hint of the warm spark that had once danced in his dark brown gaze. She smiled, slipped her arm through his and leaned against him. "How are you?"

"I'm working at getting back to myself."

"How's that coming?"

"Slowly but it is coming."

"Is there anything I can do to help?"

He shook his head. "No but thanks for asking." He sighed. "I just saw Benai leave. Is she—"

"Are you interested in her?"

"Haven't I made that clear?"

"Not lately, no."

He shrugged. "I've done my best—given the circumstances. Right now, she wouldn't want me around her."

That was true enough.

"Is she seeing anyone?"

She hesitated. "That's something you should ask her."

"I'm asking you."

"If you're really interested in her, you should make more of an effort to let her know."

"I've danced with her. I told her she looked nice."

When he'd first met Benai, the infusion of conviction in his voice had made his interest in Benai perfectly clear. "Have you asked her out?"

"No."

"Why not?"

"That would probably not be a good idea right now."

She drew away from him, studying his face. "Why not?"

"I'm having a difficult time dealing with the new me. I feel angry most of the time. When I'm not angry, I feel lost and alone. If I asked her out now...when we danced, I just wanted to rip her clothes off in the middle of the room and expose that delicious skin of hers. It was so hard to resist the urge. It was a relief when Randall asked to cut in."

She released a sigh. So that explained his failure to finish the dance with Benai. "She doesn't think you're interested."

She saw a hint of annoyance in his gaze before he exploded to his feet. "What the hell does she want from me?" He paced the length of the room. "I made my interest clear the night we met."

"But you haven't followed up since then."

He stopped in front of her and glared down at her. "You told me she needed time. I gave her time. Now you're blaming me because she's insecure?"

She felt the rage just below the surface. She suspected the only thing that kept it in check with her was the fact that she was Layton's wife. He was right. He wasn't ready to date Benai. But his anger gave her hope that when he was more himself, he would prove to Benai he was worth whatever effort or patience she extended on his behalf.

She reached up and cupped both hands over his clenched right fist. "I'm not blaming you. I'm just telling you that a woman needs assurances, Bancroft—just as men sometimes do. Just go and give her reason to hope. Tell her you're not yourself right now and ask her if you can call her in a few weeks."

He narrowed his gaze. "Why should I? I thought she might be good for Brandon."

"But?"

"But what?"

"He's not interested?"

He shrugged. "I don't know."

"You don't know? You two are twins—identical twins."

"Yes, we're physically identical but where it really counts—spirit-wise—he and Hawk are the twins. They've always been far closer than he and I have been."

"Does that bother you?"

"No. Why should it? I'm not saying we're not close. We are probably closer than a lot of twins are but he and Hawk are just closer."

"Then I should ask Layton if Brandon is interested in Benai?"

"I doubt Hawk is going to be in the mood to talk about anything but sex with you for a long time."

A rush of heat burned her cheeks. "Fine. Maybe Brandon's interested and maybe he's not."

"Your friend is a big girl. Maybe you should allow her to pick her own lovers."

Oh he was just oozing with charm. No wonder Benai was turned off. "Two things, Bancroft. First, she's a woman, not a girl. Second, you're the one who came in here to talk about her. If you're going to be rude, you can just take your sorry ass the hell out of here right now!"

For a moment, he stared at her, his dark gaze cold and hard. Oh hell. He was going to snap at her. And if Layton found out their wedding reception was going to turn ugly.

He sucked in a quick breath, clenched his right hand into a fist but remained silent.

She relaxed. "You're still interested in her. Aren't you?"

"What makes you think that?"

She squeezed his hand. "You wouldn't be this angry if you weren't interested in her." She lifted his hand and pressed her lips against his fist. "I know this is a difficult time for you, Bancroft, but like you, Benai's worth a little effort. If you just extend yourself, I know you won't be sorry."

He swore softly and pulled his hand free. "Maybe I don't agree, Tempest."

She rose to face him, a tight smile on her face. "Fine! You're not the only fish in the damned sea."

"What the hell is that supposed to mean? If she has so many damn fish swimming in her sea, why is she here alone?"

"You're here alone as well! And maybe she's here alone because she was foolish enough to think you might actually have meant what you said to her! How was she supposed to know she couldn't believe a word you said to her when you implied she took your breath away?"

She watched his gaze narrow and his lips tighten. She'd hit a nerve. The Grayhawks prided themselves on their honesty. "Are you calling me a liar, Tempest?"

"No! I'm just reminding you, that like any other single, attractive woman, she has options. She doesn't have to settle."

"Are you saying she'd be settling with me?"

"I know most women would consider you quite a catch."

"You're damned right they would."

And he was modest too. She nodded. "I know they would but you're not exactly at your best these days, are you?"

She watched the play of emotions in his eyes and was pleased that he showed no inclination to challenge her assertion that Benai was attractive. He had clearly thought so the night they met. And if the brief glimpse of fear she saw in his gaze was any indicator, he still thought so.

She moistened her lips and went on. "Maybe she'll still be free when you come back to your senses or, more likely, maybe by then someone who knows a good thing when he sees it will have swooped in and made off with her. Then he'll be the one who'll be undressing her and exposing that delicious skin of hers — which will be forever off limits to you."

His lip curled and he glared at her.

She shrugged. "In fact, there's an accountant I know who's had his eye on her for a while now and — "

"And if he wants to keep both of his eyes in working order, he'd do well to keep them off her!"

"Why should he?"

"Let him get too close and you'll both find out!" He snapped and stormed out of the room, slamming the door behind him.

Yes! That was more like it. Now she had to convince Benai to bear with Bancroft's black moods and sudden rages. She picked up the cordless phone on the nightstand and punched out Benai's cell number. She answered on the third ring. "Hello?"

"Nai! Bancroft was just in here and I know it might not seem like it but believe me, he's interested."

There was a long pause before Benai responded. "Temp, I don't know. I mean he didn't seem the least bit — "

"Just bear with him, Nai. He's dark and angry right now but that will change if you give him a chance. He might be a little cold and snappy — "

"Might be? Temp, he's colder than a block of dry ice and each time our gazes meet, he looks as if he has a grudge against me. Why would I want to put myself through that?"

"Where are you?"

"I'm in the foyer."

"The foyer?"

"Yes. I'm getting ready to leave."

"Look, Nai, I know you deserve better than what Bancroft is capable of giving you now but he'll be worth the effort. Take it from me, the darkness, while a little disturbing, can yield unexpected, sweet dividends. Layton was a great lover before but he's even better now. Under all the darkness, Bancroft is a warm, passionate man. And I know he's interested in you. If you'd seen the look in his eyes when I told him he wasn't the only fish in your sea and he'd better get his act together—"

"Temp! You didn't!"

She laughed at the horror in Benai's voice. "Oh yes, I did and I know he got the hint. If I were you, I'd expect him to come calling in a few days."

"A few days? Oh hell, Temp. Here he comes."

"Who?"

"*Him!*" Benai hissed the word.

"Bancroft?"

"Yes."

Oh boy was he interested. Yes! Hearing the uncertainly in Benai's voice, she frowned, then tensed as she heard Bancroft speak.

"When you're through with your call, would you dance with me, Benai?"

"I was about to get my coat and leave."

"Dance with me first."

Tempest bit her lip, afraid the lack of warmth in his voice would make Benai refuse. *Say yes. Please.*

"I...well. I have to go, Temp. Bancroft's here and he's asked me to dance with him."

"Rock his world, girl," she said and ended the call.

She was sitting on the bed sniffing her wrist after having applied Lelia's balm, when the bedroom door opened.

She looked up and smiled.

Layton closed and locked the door before turning to face her. "You're smiling. Happy to see me?"

She bolted off the bed and rushed across the room to link her arms around his neck. "Yes, yes and yes!"

He wrapped his arms around her waist and nuzzled her neck. She felt him stiffen before he lifted his head. "You're wearing lover's balm."

She nodded. "Lelia made it for me. She said it would make you go wild."

"Did she?"

"Yes." She stroked her fingers through the hair at his nape. "Will it?"

"I guess you'll find out tonight."

She shook her head. "I have a better idea. Why don't we find out now?"

His breathing quickened. "You said you didn't want our first time as man and wife to be quick."

"I've been thinking. Why should we rush?"

His eyes darkened. "Why indeed? Randall says the crew of his private jet is at our disposal until tomorrow night."

"Great. Then let's get this honeymoon started early."

"Now you're talking!"

He quickly removed her wedding dress, ignoring her admonition to be careful of the pearl buttons.

"Layton! If you ruin it—"

"I'll have another one made," he promised and continued with his careless removal.

When she stood in her blue bra he parted her legs, eased her against the closed door, bared his cock and thrust it into her.

As she felt his hard, thick cock tunneling quickly into her slick pussy, she cupped his face in her hands and stared up into his eyes. Seeing the hint of darkness in his gaze, she shivered. Even as he lost some of the inner darkness, his lovemaking during the last few weeks had grown more intense. Sex was now sometimes a silken thrust away from being almost as painful as it was fulfilling. Almost—except that no matter how dark his mood, there was always an underlying tenderness to his lovemaking which ensured that any pain was brief and followed by incredible joy.

She had quickly learned she wouldn't have it any other way. "Oh Layton! I love you so much!"

"Prove it. Fuck me," he ordered, bending his head to devour her lips.

Meeting him thrust for thrust, she did her best to obey.

Enjoy an excerpt from:
LOVE OUT LOUD

"So you don't have a *sheenea*?"

"No. I don't."

Good. "They're both sweet, romantic concepts, Randall."

He shrugged. "My family believes in a long line of love concept. We don't always fall in love quickly or easily but when we do fall in love, we don't stray."

"What more could a woman ask from a man?"

"Some prefer money to love," he said coolly.

"You have that as well."

"I wasn't always wealthy."

She reacted to the bitterness in his voice. "That mattered to someone you cared about?"

His jaw clenched. "We were discussing Bancroft."

So his personal life was off limits. "Yes. You were going to tell me how he lost his spiritual center."

"It started when Rissa, Brandon's *sheenea*, was murdered. We all hurt with Brandon and tried to help him work through his grief. After two years, Layton decided we needed to do something more to help him dissipate some of his grief."

"Couldn't he see a therapist?"

"It's not always easy to find a therapist who understands and respects our beliefs. Besides, Tempest might have mentioned that Declan has a healing touch."

"A healing touch? You mean he can heal people like a doctor?"

"He can't heal physical ailments but often he can help with emotional ones. Layton and Bancroft decided Brandon's emotional pain was too much for Declan to handle alone. Between the three of them, they helped Brandon rid himself of enough of his grief to help him regain his spiritual center. In the process, the three of them absorbed most of the dark, negative energy, which had been consuming him.

"As a healer, Declan was used to absorbing others' dark pain. Tempest's love and support provided an outlet for Layton's because she is Layton's *sheenea*. That left Bancroft. He has neither a *sheenea* nor a woman with whom he had a close enough emotional tie who can help him as Tempest did Layton. He's been left to struggle alone."

He raised his lids and looked at her. "Could you…"

She sighed at the pain she saw in his gaze. "I feel bad for Bancroft, Randall, but Tempest was able to help Layton and bear with the darkness in him because of her vested emotional interest in him. She loves him. I don't have any such vested interest in Bancroft. I never have."

He raked a hand through his hair. "Forgive me. I had no right to ask. It's just that he's in such pain and there's nothing we can do to help him."

"Declan can't help?"

"Croft has abilities of his own and each time Declan has tried, Croft rebuffs him. He erects mental barriers Declan can't penetrate."

She unfolded her legs and scooted across the sofa cushion to stroke a finger down his clenched right hand. "I'm not his *sheenea*, Randall. I can't help him. The darkness in him is a little…frightening."

"You'd be perfectly safe with him."

"Then why did you feel the need to rescue me?"

He pulled his hand away from her. "You weren't in any danger from him. I didn't *rescue* you."

"Okay, why did you…intervene when we were dancing?"

"Although you weren't in any danger, I could see you weren't comfortable dancing with him. You were a guest in my home so I needed to make sure you were as comfortable as possible."

"Why did you follow us into the hall?"

"I suspected you didn't want to be alone with him."

"Thanks for explaining why he's so different now."

"He won't always be so dark, Benai. When he's not—"

"I'll be very happy for him but I think I've made it clear that he's not the brother I'm interested in, Randall." She placed her hand over his.

He shook his head and withdrew it. "This was a mistake."

She felt as if he'd slashed ice water on her. "No, it wasn't."

"I shouldn't be here with you like this."

"Like what? We're talking, Randall, not making out."

"The conversation is going in directions it shouldn't."

"Why not if we both want it?" She placed a hand on his arm. "Or are you implying I'm flattering myself to think you share my interest?"

"I'm not implying anything." He glanced at his watch. "Damn. It's after eleven."

"Do you turn into a pumpkin at twelve?"

"Not tonight."

"Good. You haven't answered my question."

He rose. "I can't afford to get personal or intimate with you."

"Why not?"

"I have to go."

She stared up at him. "Randall—"

"I'd better go now, Benai before…"

She placed a hand on his thigh. "Before what?"

He stepped away from her touch. "Please don't make this any harder for me."

"It's not as if there was ever anything between Bancroft and me, Randall—"

"He thinks there is so I can't do this."

"Okay. I'll see you out." She rose. She reached for the bowtie hanging from his breast pocket.

When he reached for it, she shook her head. "I think I'll keep it as a souvenir."

He shrugged. "Fine. Keep it if you like."

"I'd rather keep you here."

"That's not going to happen." He turned and walked away.

She lightly tied the bowtie around her neck before she followed him to the apartment door.

He sighed and turned to stare down at her. "Good night."

She moistened her lips and placed a hand on his arm. "What about our date to see your pictures?"

"Give me your email address and I'll send them to you."

She placed her other hand on his chest and leaned close to him, staring up at him with her lips parted. "That wasn't the deal, Randall."

He stared at her mouth for several moments. He touched the bowtie around her neck before he sucked in a breath. "That's the way it has to be."

She slipped her hands across his chest. "So I shouldn't expect anymore cozy dinners alone with you?"

"You have no idea how hard this is for me." He closed his hands around her wrists and held her hands away from his body. "Please don't touch me like that."

"It's not nearly as intimately as I'd like to touch you, Randall."

Still holding her wrists, he leaned close, his lips parting and his head bending.

She closed her eyes and waited to feel his lips against hers.

Enjoy an excerpt from:
FULL BODIED CHARMER

∞

When Rick pulled into the Fourth Street parking lot, he immediately noticed Jennifer sitting in her car. He parked a few spaces over and walked to her vehicle. She watched his approach. When he neared her car, she smiled at him.

He blinked and took a deep breath. Damn, but she had an incredible smile and absolutely beautiful eyes. And she knew how to dress, he thought as she got out of her car. She had on a pretty pink dress that provided an intriguing view of her ample cleavage. Her breasts were delightfully large.

There were few things sexier than a beautiful woman with big tits. What would it be like to touch and kiss those luscious looking mounds and tongue her nipples? His cock stirred and he found it difficult to tear his gaze away from her breasts and look into her eyes. Once he had, he could see she was aware of the effect the sight of her breasts was having on his libido.

Her smile was wondrous: shy, yet tinged with a hint of confidence he found incredibly alluring.

"Hi." She spoke first and widened her smile.

He felt his own lips turning up in a smile and he eagerly reached for her hand. "Hi, Jennifer. Nice to see you again."

"It's nice to see you again, too." Her voice and gaze were warm and welcoming.

He stared down into her eyes. Why would such a lovely, sexy woman have to buy a date? There must be any number of men waiting to take her to bed. He sure as hell did.

He released her hand and nodded towards his car. "Is it okay if we take my car?"

"What's the matter? Don't trust a woman driver?" She arched her brows, grinning up at him.

He swallowed quickly. If she kept smiling at him like that, he was liable to sweep her into his arms, slam his cock into her and fuck her breathless right there in the parking lot.

"It's not that," he denied. He didn't quite trust himself to keep his hands off her if she drove instead of him.

"I was teasing. I have no problem with going in your car."

"Good." He resisted the urge to offer her his arm and they walked to his car together.

In the confines of his car, it was difficult to think of anything other than how close she was and how much he'd like to touch her. *Okay, Rick. Get real. You are not going to take her to bed.* What he needed to do was talk so he wouldn't sit there fantasizing about her. "What kind of music do you like?" he asked.

"I like nearly all types of music, but my absolute favorites are blues and mellow jazz. I "I like nearly all types of music, but my absolute favorites are blues and mellow jazz. I like to close my eyes and sway to music I can feel through my bones and all the way down to my soul."

He bit back the urge to offer to take her to his favorite jazz club. They spent the rest of the twenty-minute drive to the River Rooms talking about their individual jazz and blues favorites. When they arrived, he held the passenger door open for her and offered her his arm. She gave him a breathtaking smile and slipped her arm through his.

He had to look away to keep from staring down into her cleavage. When they were seated in one of the high backed booths, he made no attempt to look away from her.

After sipping at drinks, they ordered their dinner. Used to women who ordered tiny salads with low-calorie dressing and diet drinks, he listened in amazement as she ordered a salad with regular dressing—to be followed by veal scaloppini.

She clearly enjoyed her food, and he enjoyed watching her savor every bite.

"What sort of things do you like to do?"

She smiled. "I like sitting in jazz clubs, walking barefoot along the beach in the moonlight, dancing on a boat, and sweating to the oldies."

"Sweating to the oldies?"

"You sound surprised. What? You think full-figured gals are all couch potatoes?"

"No," he denied, feeling the heat rise up the back of his neck. "Of course not."

She tilted her head to one side and her thick, dark hair cascaded against one shoulder. She shook her head. "Why don't I believe you?"

"I have no idea," he said wearily.

"Well, this full-figured or size-positive gal works out regularly. All my...parts work perfectly."

He allowed his gaze to flick briefly over her. Maybe that explained why she seemed so...solid. Granted, she was much larger than any woman he'd ever been out with. Nevertheless, she was as sexy as hell with it, especially her delectable-looking cleavage. A man could probably bury his face between those beautiful breasts and never want to surface again. He felt his cock stirring and shifted uncomfortably in his seat.

"Oh, I'll just bet they do." The comment surprised him and if the arching of her brows were an indicator, her too. "It might interest you to know that all my...parts work rather well, too. "

She treated him to one of those delicious smiles of hers and he sighed. Damn, it was going to be a long, frustrating night.

They talked sports over dinner. He found that she was a big baseball and basketball fan.

"No hockey or football?"

She shook her head and swallowed a mouthful of her veal scaloppini. "No, but I have to admit I do occasionally turn on football with no sound."

"Why no sound?"

"Well, I'm not really into football."

"Then why watch it?"

"I like watching all those guys with nice tight buns running around." She bit her lip and laughed, a warm, sweet sound that seemed to caress his ears. "I've shocked you."

"No. Believe me, it takes more than that to shock me."

"Then what's that look about?"

"It's just that you're different from any woman I've been out with."

"Size wise?"

"Yes," he admitted, "but that's not the only way you're different." He paused, not sure how to put his thoughts into words. "You're different in a...very nice way."

"Thank you. So are you."

"Me? How?"

She sipped her drink, then ran the tip of her tongue along her bottom lip, an action he found highly erotic. "Well, you're blond, for one thing. "

He stared at her. "And?"

"Well, you know what they say about blonds," she said, widening her eyes.

"Being dumb?" he asked, the heat rising up the back of his neck again. "That's what they say about blonde women, not blond men."

"Well, if you say they only mean it for women—" she said, her lips curving in an enchanting smile.

"Are you by any chance implying that I'm a dumb blond?"

"No. I did say you were different, didn't I?"

"So you did."

Both smiling, they finished their main course in silence. He watched as she slowly ate a piece of cheesecake, clearly savoring each bite. It was a nice change to be out with a woman who didn't make him feel like a pig because he wanted something more substantial than a big bowl of lettuce for dinner.

Noticing his close scrutiny, a faint hint of color touched her cheeks. "Would you like a bite?"

About to shake his head, he nodded instead. "Just to see what all the oohing and aahing is about."

She looked around for a clean fork.

"That one will do," he told her.

She held up her fork. "This one?"

"Yes, assuming, of course, you're not poisoned or have a really bad cold."

"No poison or cold germs." She used her fork to offer him a piece of the cheesecake. He leaned forward. She put the fork in his mouth. Their gazes met and locked. He swallowed the small piece of cake without really tasting it.

"So? Do you like it?" Her voice sounded slightly breathless.

"Yes...I like yo—it."

She smiled and looked at him from beneath lowered lids. "I like yo—it too."

He sat back. "Do you mind if I ask your age?"

She shook her head. "Twenty-nine."

"Really? You look younger."

"And do you look younger than you are?"

"I don't know. I'm forty."

"Really?" She widened her eyes. "I would have sworn you weren't a day over thirty-nine years and three hundred and sixty days or so."

They laughed together and he decided she was even prettier when she laughed.

They talked sports for a while longer before he asked her if she'd like to dance.

She nodded and smiled. "Yes. They're playing one of my favorite songs."

He listened and realized the song in question was the instrumental version of Billy Joel's *Just The Way You Are*. "I like it too."

As they danced, she burrowed against him, resting her cheek against his shoulder and moving her hands in small, caressing motions against his back. He found that he liked the weight of her body against his. The feel of her big breasts against his chest caused his cock to slowly come to life. Oh, damn! He drew his lower body away from hers. He hoped she hadn't felt the beginnings of his desire. When she lifted her head and looked up at him, he saw the awareness of his yearning in her gaze.

"I...I'm sorry, " he said. "It's been awhile and I..."

"No need to apologize," she told him.

To his amazement, she moved her lower body against his and there was no hiding his growing erection from her. He wasn't in the mood to be teased then sent on his way to take a cold shower.

He dropped his arms and stepped away from her. "Ah, we should go."

She shrugged. "Okay. If that's what you want."

"It's what I need to do."

She sighed. "I've shocked you again. Haven't I? You expected me to be coy or maybe to pretend to be coy?"

Not exactly, but he also hadn't expected her to press against his hardening cock either. "I don't and didn't expect anything in particular. We agreed to spend a few hours together for charity. We've done that."

There was no mistaking the flush on her cheeks. "So we have. Well, let's go."

He knew she'd misunderstood his meaning and probably thought he hadn't enjoyed their evening together. He had, but he decided to let it pass.

At the Fourth Street lot, he insisted on following her in his car to make sure she arrived safely home.

"That's not necessary," she told him, her voice cool.

"Maybe not, but I'd like to…unless you really object."

"No. Fine."

Thirty minutes later, he parked his car behind hers and walked her into her apartment building. They rode the elevator in silence. At her apartment door, they stood staring at each other for several moments before she spoke. "I'm sorry you didn't have a better time."

She sounded shy and a little uncertain. He knew the feeling. He wanted to kiss her, but he didn't want to give her the wrong idea. "What are you talking about? I had a great time."

"You did?"

"Yes. I did."

"Oh, good. So did I."

She smiled that amazing smile of hers that turned her pretty face into a beautiful one. Caution be damned. He had to have at least one chaste kiss before they said goodbye.

He brushed his fingers against her cheek before bending his head. He intended to peck at her mouth briefly, but the moment their lips met, he felt a rush of desire. Fighting to control it, he pressed three quick kisses against her lips before he lifted his head and looked down at her.

She kept her eyes closed for several seconds before looking up at him with her wide silver gaze. He stared back. The hint of red on her cheeks served to make her even more alluring. He wanted another kiss, maybe several more—longer and deeper.

He slipped his hands under the long, dark curtain of her hair to cup her face in his palms. He bent his head slowly, giving her ample time to object. She gave him a shy, sweet smile, closed her eyes, and lifted her face.

He brushed his lips gently against hers, nipped at her mouth until she sucked in a breath and parted her lips. Then he kissed her. Her lips, soft and warm, clung to his. He kissed her hungrily, savoring the taste and texture of her mouth. He sucked at her tongue and slipped an arm around her waist to draw her body against his.

She shivered and leaned closer. He deepened the kiss, moving his hand from her cheek to close his fingers in the long dark hair at the nape of her neck. Her breasts pressing against his chest heightened his desire. With one final long kiss, he reluctantly drew away from her. He was so aroused his cock felt as if it weighed a ton.

She opened her eyes and they silently stared at each other. Her cheeks were flushed, her beautiful silver eyes bright, and her lips still slightly parted. He wondered if she, like he, wanted the kissing to go on and on until it went beyond the kissing stage. And that would not do. He'd had a surprisingly great time with her and done his bit for charity. Now it was time to get the hell out of there before he lost his head completely.

"Would you like to come in for coffee?"

The question didn't surprise him nearly as much as his instinctive desire to seize the opportunity to get her alone behind closed doors and maybe into bed. After her eager response to his kisses, he had a feeling she might be receptive to allowing him to spend the night. With his cock hardening at an alarming rate, he longed to take her to bed. He gazed into her eyes again and saw a complete lack of guile. She was different from the women he was used to bedding, who thought nothing of hopping into bed for a one-nighter and moving on without a single backward glance.

He smiled. "Thanks, but I'd better hit the road."

Her smile wavered for a moment before she widened it. She extended her hand. "Goodbye."

He enclosed her hand in both of his. The surge of desire he felt was so strong he dropped her hand and took several steps away from her. "Goodbye."

* * * * *

The soft jazz filling the car as Rick drove home kept thoughts of Jennifer uppermost in his mind. He couldn't stop thinking about her or their evening together. Recalling her response to his touch and kisses made his cock throb. What the hell had possessed him to turn down her invitation for "coffee"? It wasn't as if he'd pressured her in any way. She had freely extended the invitation he'd so badly wanted to accept.

Halfway home, he decided he'd made a big mistake. She was an adult. If she wanted him to spend the night with her, why shouldn't he? With visions of her beautiful face and silver eyes spurring him on, he got off the highway at the next exit and turned his car around.

Also by Marilyn Lee

ಐ

About the Author

Marilyn Lee lives, works, and writes on the East Coast. In addition to thoroughly enjoying writing erotic romances, she enjoys roller-skating, spending time with her large, extended family, and rooting for all her hometown sports teams. Her other interests include collecting Doc Savage pulp novels from the thirties and forties and collecting Marvel comics from the seventies and eighties (particularly Thor and The Avengers). Her favorite TV shows are forensic shows, westerns (Gunsmoke and Have Gun, Will Travel are particular favors), mysteries (love the old Charlie Chan mysteries. All time favorite mystery movie is probably Dead, Again), and nearly every vampire movie or television show ever made (Forever Knight and Count Yorga, Vampire are favors). She thoroughly enjoys hearing from readers.

Marilyn welcomes comments from readers. You can find her website and email address on her author bio page at www.ellorascave.com.

Tell Us What You Think

We appreciate hearing reader opinions about our books. You can email us at Comments@EllorasCave.com.

Why an electronic book?

We live in the Information Age—an exciting time in the history of human civilization, in which technology rules supreme and continues to progress in leaps and bounds every minute of every day. For a multitude of reasons, more and more avid literary fans are opting to purchase e-books instead of paper books. The question from those not yet initiated into the world of electronic reading is simply: *Why?*

1. *Price.* An electronic title at Ellora's Cave Publishing and Cerridwen Press runs anywhere from 40% to 75% less than the cover price of the exact same title in paperback format. Why? Basic mathematics and cost. It is less expensive to publish an e-book (no paper and printing, no warehousing and shipping) than it is to publish a paperback, so the savings are passed along to the consumer.

2. *Space.* Running out of room in your house for your books? That is one worry you will never have with electronic books. For a low one-time cost, you can purchase a handheld device specifically designed for e-reading. Many e-readers have large, convenient screens for viewing. Better yet, hundreds of titles can be stored within your new library—on a single microchip. There are a variety of e-readers from different manufacturers. You can also read e-books on your PC or laptop computer. (Please note that Ellora's Cave does not endorse any specific brands.

You can check our websites at www.ellorascave.com or www.cerridwenpress.com for information we make available to new consumers.)

3. *Mobility.* Because your new e-library consists of only a microchip within a small, easily transportable e-reader, your entire cache of books can be taken with you wherever you go.

4. ***Personal Viewing Preferences.*** Are the words you are currently reading too small? Too large? Too... ANNOYING? Paperback books cannot be modified according to personal preferences, but e-books can.

5. ***Instant Gratification.*** Is it the middle of the night and all the bookstores near you are closed? Are you tired of waiting days, sometimes weeks, for bookstores to ship the novels you bought? Ellora's Cave Publishing sells instantaneous downloads twenty-four hours a day, seven days a week, every day of the year. Our webstore is never closed. Our e-book delivery system is 100% automated, meaning your order is filled as soon as you pay for it.

Those are a few of the top reasons why electronic books are replacing paperbacks for many avid readers.

As always, Ellora's Cave and Cerridwen Press welcome your questions and comments. We invite you to email us at Comments@ellorascave.com or write to us directly at Ellora's Cave Publishing Inc., 1056 Home Avenue, Akron, OH 44310-3502.

COMING TO A BOOKSTORE NEAR YOU!

ELLORA'S CAVE

Bestselling Authors Tour

UPDATES AVAILABLE AT

WWW.EllorasCave.COM

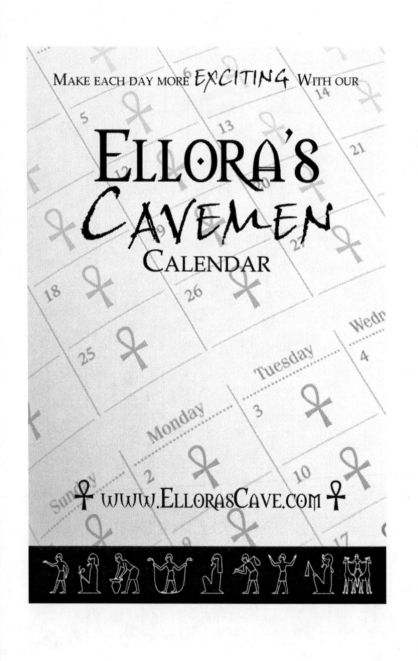

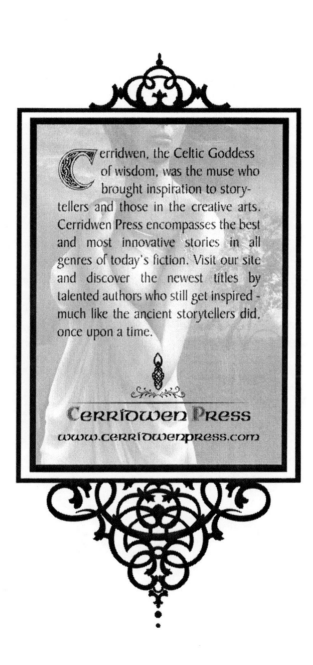

Cerridwen, the Celtic Goddess of wisdom, was the muse who brought inspiration to story-tellers and those in the creative arts. Cerridwen Press encompasses the best and most innovative stories in all genres of today's fiction. Visit our site and discover the newest titles by talented authors who still get inspired - much like the ancient storytellers did, once upon a time.

Cerridwen Press
www.cerridwenpress.com